POSER

POSER

ALISON HUGHES

ORCA BOOK PUBLISHERS

Library and Archives Canada Cataloguing in Publication

Hughes, Alison, 1966-
Poser / Alison Hughes.

Issued also in electronic formats.
ISBN 978-1-4598-0147-9

I. Title.
PS8615.U3165P68 2013   jc813'.6   c2012-907452-7

First published in the United States, 2013
Library of Congress Control Number: 2012952942

Summary: Twelve-year-old Luke has been a model for as long as he can remember,
but all he really wants to do is play hockey and eat pizza with extra cheese.

*Orca Book Publishers is dedicated to preserving the environment and has printed
this book on Forest Stewardship Council® certified paper.*

Orca Book Publishers gratefully acknowledges the support for its publishing
programs provided by the following agencies: the Government of Canada through the
Canada Book Fund and the Canada Council for the Arts, and the Province of British
Columbia through the BC Arts Council and the Book Publishing Tax Credit.

Cover design by Teresa Bubela
Cover photography by Corbis
Author photo by Barbara Heintzman

ORCA BOOK PUBLISHERS   ORCA BOOK PUBLISHERS
PO Box 5626, STN. B   PO Box 468
VICTORIA, BC CANADA   CUSTER, WA USA
v8R 6s4   98240-0468

www.orcabook.com
Printed and bound in Canada.

16   15   14   13   •   4   3   2   1

*For my pack—Mitchell, Kate, Ben
and Sam—and for my parents,
Laurie and Claudette.*

CHAPTER ONE

I AM SPARED AT LEAST ONE MAJOR HUMILIATION

I probably shouldn't start this story with a rant. I probably should try to be dignified, welcome you in and let you get to know me before I start complaining. But the whole argument over the title of this book was just so typical of the kinds of hassles in my life that it's as good a place as any to begin. It was a close call, but I sort of won.

Now, you might think the title of a book is a smallish thing, just a few words to grab your attention and get you to take it off the shelf. That's what I used to think. But I've discovered that a title can actually be kind of important. In only a few words, it can cleverly summarize the whole feel of the story. Or it can suck and make you look like an idiot.

So here's the thing: Mom and Aunt Macy (especially Aunt Macy) decided that the book *had* to be called *Beauty Boy*. Yes, *Beauty Boy*. Welcome to my nightmare. "Beauty Boy" (BB for short) has been their nickname for me since I was a fat baby barely holding up my own head and drooling on the props in the infant photo shoots. I'd made the cover of *Baby Show* and done the Dribbleez Diapers ad campaign by the time I was eight months old. Are you impressed? I didn't think so. But let me just say that it was a big deal in the baby-modeling industry at the time.

Anyway, Aunt Macy argued long and loud for the title to be *Beauty Boy*. And believe me, nobody can argue longer and louder. She wore everybody down until we were all ready to agree to anything if she would just stop.

I think that's a technique actual torturers use.

Anyway, Aunt Macy said the title *Beauty Boy* would intrigue you, make you curious, make you want to read on. You know: *Who is this boy? What's with the beauty? What can it mean?*

I told them they might as well put a *FREAK* sign on me and parade me all over town. I told them kids would laugh when they saw that title. Or they would feel uncomfortable, or worse, they'd pity me. And pity isn't supposed to happen until later in the book.

Finally, the editor did something amazing. She took my side! She actually stood up to Macy. She told me I was overdoing it a bit on the pity/humiliation thing, but she agreed that *Beauty Boy* was too weird for a title. And just like that, unbelievably, I was saved. The title issue was wide open.

I wanted the title to be *True Confessions of a Serial Liar: The Life and Lies of Luke Spinelli*. That's pretty good, isn't it? Dignified. Adult. Gives you some actual info too.

Everyone said it was too many words. Actually, my Aunt Macy said, "Oh, jeez. You ever *read* a book? How many words you think they can fit on a little cover?" More on Macy later, although that gives you a bit of an idea of her.

So then I thought maybe something like *Framed!* (maybe with The Luke Spinelli Story in very small print underneath). Short, punchy, bit of a double meaning there. That turned out to be the problem though. While I've been "framed" as in thousands and thousands of photos, I've never been "framed" as in a crime. Hey, I'm only twelve. Give me time.

Bottom line is that everybody thought *Framed!* was misleading. Also, between you and me, I could see them doing some lame book cover with me in a fake striped jailbird suit, holding a frame around my face, with sort of "Aw, shucks" look on my face. I would have *really* hated that.

Anyway, when Macy and Mom shot that one down, I tried *Slightly Out of Focus: The Luke Spinelli Story*; *Forcing the Smile: The Luke Spinelli Story*; *Say "Cheese!": The Luke Spinelli Story* and a few others I can't remember right now. Bang, bang, bang. Shot down, every last one of them.

And then, out of the blue, the editor, who was looking very tired by this point and was possibly regretting having agreed to the whole thing, suggested *Poser*. I jumped at it. A one-word title that isn't completely embarrassing? Where's the downside? Mom agreed, and we gradually, eventually, wore Aunt Macy down. Three against one are good odds.

So *Poser* it is. At least you won't have to cover it up with something else when you read it.

You *are* going to read it, aren't you?

It's a good story, and it's true. Except the parts where I'm lying. But the thing is, you'll *know* I'm lying. True stories are pretty rare. So you can safely assume I have no superpowers and that I'm not a vampire, werewolf, extraterrestrial or ninja. There aren't any intergalactic laser battles or a frantic race to save the world from armies of killer robots.

Actually, come to think of it, maybe the truth kind of sucks.

But hey, nobody dies. I'll tell you that up front. And that's a promise. I hate books like that. They get you all attached to this character (like, say, me) and then they kill him off? Or the guy's mom or buddy or something? What's with that? Nope, nobody dies. Not even the small-part people, like the shy girl in class or the lady who runs the video store. Nobody. All living, all the time.

And another bonus: there's no heavy moral in here. No moral at all, in fact. Not even about the lying. In fact, lying saves my life many times in this story, so I'm quite a big fan of it. Anyway, it will become very, *very* clear to you that I'm the last person you should look to for life lessons.

So here's a quick plot summary: our story starts out with some minor cringeworthy events, morphs into a gigantic monster lie, and some more humiliation, then there's a really excruciatingly embarrassing part, and then, just when you have your fingers pressed to your mouth and think it can't get any worse…well, I won't give it all away.

I've probably said enough. Everybody says I talk too much. Although on the plus side, people also say I get less annoying the more you get to know me.

My friends mostly just tell me to shut up. So, while you're reading, you can say, "Shut *up*, Spin" just like they would.

5

Or how about this: I get annoying, and you just shut the book, count to ten, get a snack or take a break or whatever, then open it up again.

I'll be here.

CHAPTER TWO

WE BEGIN WITH FAKE-RUNNING (IF YOUR THIGH DOESN'T BURN, YOU AREN'T DOING IT RIGHT)

I spend a lot of my life posing.

I don't mean the leaning-in-a-cool-way-against-your-locker-to-impress-the-girls kind of posing. I mean actual posing, with lights and cameras and fake smiles.

The fake "just hanging out" hands-in-the-pockets pose, the fake "point into the distance" pose, the fake "aren't we all having fun" belly-laugh pose, the fake-serious soulful look off to the side, the fake-formal hand-in-one-pocket dress-clothes pose...I could go on and on. I've done them all.

The photographers say things like, "Hey, *I* know, let's pretend you see something funny over there, and you're pointing it out to your friend!"

I'd rather they just said, "Hey, kid, fake-laugh and point." We'd all get out of there a lot quicker.

But in my experience, photographers like to chat, like to feel they're having a *creative experience*. Making a real *connection*. Buddy, you're shooting a *flyer*. Somebody, maybe, will glance at it for two seconds, then shove it into a recycling bin. Get the kid models to look cute in cheap clothes. There's your creativity.

Anyway, the pose I hate the most is the one I'm doing right now. Fake-running.

It's like this: you're usually wearing cheap, no-brand athletic wear and ten-dollar runners that are *never* the right size, you're fake-grinning at some point ahead of you or over your shoulder, you pretend you're starting to run, and then you *freeze*. Just like that.

And you hold it for however long the photographer wants, while you get hotter and hotter and your grin gets stiffer and more fake until it's more of a grimace than a smile.

Try it. You have to balance on the one leg. No cheating.

I was at the grimacing point. Out of one fake-smiling eye, I could see the girl beside me starting to shake. That'll happen when you're new to this. It's that balance leg; it gives out on you all the time when you're just starting out.

"*Hold* the pose, please," barked the photographer as the girl put her foot down for a second. The one that was supposed to be up fake-running.

This photographer was new. He probably described himself as "good with kids" to get this job. If by that he meant using vicious sarcasm and fake sweetness to try to get us to smile for the two seconds he needs us to, then he's *great* with kids.

My leg was starting to burn, too, and they were going to need a no-blur lens the way the girl beside me was shaking now. *Hang in there, little buddy*, I thought grimly. A second shoot with this guy would not be pretty.

"No, it's not working," snapped the photographer, stepping back from the camera. "Just relax for a second; let me think."

He ran his fingers through his thinning hair, looked around and lit a cigarette.

That, I thought, *is against the building rules and against the terms of our contracts*. There was a clause in there on secondhand smoke; I was sure of it. But I wasn't really in a position to argue the man down. Wearing a pink golf shirt and turquoise-and-pink-striped shorts kind of undermines your authority.

I just wanted this to be over.

"He's meeeean," whispered the girl beside me, stretching her leg. She was, I guessed, about seven years old underneath her makeup. She was supposed to be my little sister or cousin or something in the shoot, although we looked nothing alike. But advertising is like that. I've had "mothers" in a shoot who were blond and barely out of their teens. Very authentic.

I once did a shoot for some real-estate brochure where I was the "kid" to two impossibly young, cute parents. I had to ride on "Dad's" shoulders while "Mom" flipped her hair and people off-camera tossed fake fall leaves at us. When I told "Dad" he had no hair on one spot of his head (which was the *truth*), he pinched my leg *hard* and never stopped smiling. Good, quality fake-family time.

Anyway, I felt bad for the girl beside me now: you could tell her shoes were too tight, she was new to the fake-running pose, and now she had to sit here breathing illegal smoke into her little lungs.

"Yep," I said, looking at the photographer frantically puffing away, "a real jerk. Nice hair though," I murmured, and she giggled. The photographer's hair, what there was of it, was practically standing on end.

He stubbed out his cigarette and walked over to us. All of a sudden, he was *super* nice.

"Okay, kids, we're going to try an over-the-shoulder look. Okay?" He spoke slowly. "Over. The. Shoulder." He demonstrated, as though he were talking to non-English speakers. "Like you're seeing something, a balloon or a bird or something, over *there*. Got it?"

Did I mention I'm twelve? If I didn't, I'm *twelve*. And I'm supposed to swivel around excitedly for balloons and birdies? Is this guy serious?

The girl and I both nodded earnestly. Basically, what I've learned in this business is to smile and nod. They don't want input. Nobody cares about your artistic vision. Just put on the cheap clothes and fake-smile over your shoulder. While fake-running.

"This is while we're in the running pose?" the girl asked. Mistake. This guy didn't want questions. He wanted smiling. He wanted nodding. I turned to her, smiling and nodding.

"Obviously," snapped the photographer.

The girl nodded. Quick learner.

The photographer motioned to an assistant who was wheeling in a huge fan and helped her position it. Great. Fake wind too.

Another woman touched up our makeup, then turned to me with a sweater. A pink one.

"Randy says we gotta put this on you." She tilted her head toward the photographer. "Just drape it over your shoulders, kinda casual and sporty, like...*that*. Cool! Awesome!"

Here's a tip. There's a big difference between what adults and kids think is "cool" and "awesome."

This was seriously lame loser-wear. If I saw a guy on the street dressed like this, I'd think he was a complete freak. I'd feel sorry for him and look away while other people pointed and laughed.

Nobody's going to see it, I reminded myself. *It's just a small, local Calgary flyer. Nobody in Edmonton will see it.*

So far, nobody other than Mom and Aunt Macy knows I'm a model. That's exactly the way I want it to stay. Most of Macy's modeling contacts are out of town. All the local companies and agencies that I used to model for years ago got fed up with being pestered by her. Fine by me. For *very* obvious reasons, I don't want people to recognize me/ ridicule me/pity me.

"Okay, guys," said Randy, his voice extra nice now. You could tell he wanted to wrap this up. "It's summer. Hot. You're just playing outside, running and…you know, just running…"

In this, Randy? Are you serious? Have you ever even been a kid?

We nodded, as if pointless fake-running was totally understandable.

"And," Randy continued, fake excitement lighting up his face, "running behind you is a big, friendly, shaggy dog! So you turn to look at it." He turned, smiling. When he turned, a roll of belly flab peeked out from under his T-shirt. His teeth were yellow. No dog would trot happily after this guy. We kept nodding.

"Okay," he snapped, all business now. "Places. Wind. Go."

We did our best fake-running and fake-grinning at the fake doggie. My balance leg and my strained face were burning when we finished.

I knew from experience that it would all look pretty natural when the flyer came out. Randy was probably better than I gave him credit for. The girl I was modeling with was a natural too. Why did that make me feel kind of sad?

I'm good at this too. I should be. I've been modeling for a looong time. Too long. I'm a semiprofessional boy model.

I don't know what that says about me.

But I'm thinking that *you're* thinking it's probably not good.

CHAPTER THREE

MACY CRANKS IT UP A WHOLE NOTHER NOTCH ON DEAD END STREET

Our end of the street has no name. We live on Cuthbert Street, and we have the address on our bills to prove it. It clearly says *Cuthbert Street* on the other end of the street, across the main road. But the only sign indicating our end of the street says *DEAD END*. Although I think about it every day, I try hard not to let that mean anything deeper.

Mom, me and Macy rent the left side of a duplex in a group of duplexes called Mayfair Estates, which makes it sound fancy schmancy. It's not. An old guy named Dan cuts the grass, and his wife plants a few scrappy flowers, but other than that, it's just duplexes.

Mom and I passed the Mayfair Estates notice board on our way home after the shoot. The same notice—the only notice—has been on there since we moved here five years ago: *Tenants MUST place garbage IN the dumpsters, not along-side, which is stricktly forbidden.* Welcome home.

Aunt Macy was on the computer when we got in. She's always on the computer. Searching for my big break: the Sears catalog, the Bay Days flyers, a Walmart ad campaign.

She swiveled around and called, "Well? How'd it go? You have fun?"

Actually, it's hard to show in writing how Macy speaks. She doesn't actually "call" like I said just now. That makes it sound like the way normal humans speak.

With Macy, it's more like yelling or shouting, with shades of bellowing. The woman is *loud.* Just imagine that EVERYTHING SHE SAYS IN HER DEEP, LOUD SMOKER'S VOICE IS ALL IN CAPITALS!!! VERY, VERY *LOUD* CAPITALS!!! Mrs. Fitzpatrick, the old, partially deaf lady who lives beside us, calls her Megaphone Macy behind her back.

And it's not just her voice. Everything about Macy is big. Freakishly big. She's over six feet tall and sort of big all around. Just like her brother. Actually, if you took that picture of my dad that's over the couch, put lots of makeup on him and a long, black, frizzy wig, you'd get Macy. That's kind of a creepy image, but you get the picture.

"I'm *starving*," I said, taking off my coat and heading to the kitchen. Mom followed me, smoothing her wispy brown hair out of her eyes.

"Me too," she said. "Hmm, what do we have?" She slipped her arm around me as we stared into the fridge. I am almost as tall as she is.

Nothing. We had nothing.

"Don't you hate it when you're starving and you look into the fridge and there's *nothing*?" I asked her. "I mean, maybe there's some ketchup and margarine, and eggs and milk and celery. But really, nothing."

I demonstrated my food-hunting strategy.

"Fridge first. If there's nothing there, I go to the cereal cupboard in search of sugary goodness." I opened it. Bran cereal and oatmeal. Nothing. I lunged across the kitchen.

"Then, in desperation, I open the spice cupboard and hunt for stray chocolate chips," I said.

Mom laughed, leaning back against the counter and crossing her arms. "Please tell me you find them every once in a while," she said.

"Not often, but sometimes. Found a hardish marshmallow once too."

"Okay, this is getting pathetic," she said. "Point taken. I'll get groceries tomorrow on my way home from work, I promise. Maybe I'll even sprinkle a few chocolate chips here and there…"

The doorbell rang. We looked at each other.

"PIZZA!" shouted Macy, giving us a wink as she stomped to the door.

We watched in amazement as she paid the pizza guy and brought in a huge, steaming box.

Now, I'm guessing that for most normal families, having pizza is probably a normal thing to do occasionally. Not for us. Our house has a strict no-fun-food policy. I'm already big for my age, and everybody knows the camera adds pounds. And while Mom and Macy never use the word "diet," they take healthy eating very seriously. At least, Mom does. I'm sure Macy secretly gorges on burgers and fries.

Mom makes very healthy, very serious food. We have lots of vegetables and grilled fish. We have bread and pasta occasionally, and fruit for snacking. We almost never have pizza. Or chips. Or soda.

"This is fun, Macy!" Mom said. "What's the occasion?"

"Oh, just thought it would be a nice change. And I've got something to tell you guys after."

I dug in.

Suggestion: those of you normal folks out there who get pizza every other day, give it up for a few months. Then when you come back to it, you will truly appreciate it for the cheesy miracle it is. I closed my eyes and just experienced the pizza.

I left it to Mom to tell Macy about the shoot. I hate talking about shoots after they're over. What's the point? It's like those kids at school who come out of a test, start flipping through their notes and go, "Whatcha get for number four?" At that point, I'm trying to *forget* number four. After a test, the last thing I want to think about is the test. The point, people, is that it's *over*.

Anyway, Macy is my agent, so I guess it's technically part of her job to ask a million questions after a shoot if she's not there herself. She likes to keep on top of things.

She's got an incredible memory, I'll give her that. She remembers the names of every kid I've ever had a shoot with, all the photographers, even the assistants. She remembers the *clothes*. She'll be trying to get me to remember a shoot from years ago, and she'll say, "C'mon, Beauty Boy, it was with Dylan and Remy. Remember? The acid-wash jean pantsuit with the striped red T-shirt shoot? Remember?" Actually, Macy, I've spent years trying to erase the acid-wash jean pantsuit from my mind.

Macy and Mom finally finished talking about the shoot.

"So, what did you want to tell us?" I asked through a mouth full of pizza. I'd been wondering. I was getting suspicious. Macy generally did things for a reason.

"Okay," said Macy, smiling and pushing her plate away. "Here goes: I'm cranking the agent thing up a whole nother notch! I'm starting a company, an official modeling agency—it's called Models by Macy." She spread her huge hands wide, like she was showing how the name would look up in lights.

"Serious agent stuff. Website, online profiles of models, big-name clients, the works! And don't think I'm going to forget you, Beauty Boy! You're my biggest star!"

As far as I knew, I was Macy's only client. Her only star.

"Now," she said, getting businesslike, "it's time to crank *your* career up a whole nother notch too, BB. You're thirteen in June, so we gotta be shifting into teen stuff. With your talent and looks, you deserve a national campaign! Maybe commercials! International stuff! Who knows? Maybe even TV, movies, DISNEY! I got Big Plans, BB! Whaddaya think?"

She looked at me expectantly.

What did I think? What did I *think*?

I was frozen. Horror has a way of doing that to a guy. I couldn't imagine anything worse than Macy's taking things up a whole nother notch. I could barely control Macy on the previous notch. But now that notch felt safe. I felt my feet and hands go cold, and my head start to pound. I swallowed carefully.

Just pass out, I thought to myself. *Just pass out right now, and you won't have to deal with this.*

I didn't pass out. Not even a wobble. Have you ever noticed how your body sometimes ignores simple instructions that your brain sends out, like "Pass out right now"?

I looked wildly over at Mom, but she was smiling at Macy. Mom loves Macy. She says she's got a good heart. They've been friends forever. Macy has helped us through some tough times. But the point right now was this disaster, this crisis, this plan that would ruin my whole life.

"Macy!" Mom said. "Models by Macy sounds wonderful! Have you got any leads on new clients?"

They chatted away as I slowly died inside. Well, I felt very, very cold, anyway. My mind was racing. Commercials? I hated commercials. They got in the way of watching a good hockey game.

I imagined having to look straight into a camera and say stupid catchphrases like "Chewy, gooey goodness!" or "Betalax: for real relief you can trust" or "Bursting with berry, berry good taste!"

I could not bear it.

As I stumbled away on shaky legs, Macy grabbed my arm. She's got a grip like a linebacker.

"Hey, not so fast, buster!" she laughed. "You gotta look at my new promo stuff! C'mon."

She dragged me over to the computer and pulled up her website. A creamy background displayed swirly purple lettering: *Models by Macy*. There was a glamorous picture of someone in the top corner.

I squinted at it. Was that supposed to be Macy? She was wearing a ton of makeup and looked about fifty pounds thinner. I guess it really was Macy, because underneath the photo, it said *Macy Spinelli, M.A., Professional Modeling Agent and Promoter.*

"M.A.?" I asked. As far as I knew, Macy had barely finished high school.

"Modeling Agent," Macy said over her shoulder. "You gotta have letters, otherwise people don't think you're legit. Wait a sec." She clicked some more, pulling down the *Clients* menu.

"Now, it's not final yet. I'm just kind of drafting it up, but HEEEERE he is! Here's BEAUTY BOY!" she shouted.

There I was. A huge, fake-smiling portfolio picture introduced a long, glowing write-up of all my accomplishments. Everything. Even my winning the Eastside Mall Kutest Kid Kompetition when I was five. There were endless scroll-down pictures from what appeared to be every shoot I had ever done. Fake-laughing, fake-running, fake-pointing, I just kept on coming.

I closed my eyes long before we scrolled to the end and slid weakly to my knees beside the computer desk.

Nobody noticed; Macy and Mom were busy pointing and reminiscing.

"Oh, remember that one? With that little train engineer's cap and the overalls? Sooo cute!"

"Here's BB looking all smarty-pants in glasses and a tie! The Serious Students campaign for *Know-It-All* magazine."

And on and on and on.

I sat crumpled on the floor.

There I was. One Google search, and anyone could see me. Anyone. Like, for example, my entire grade-seven class at Leonard Petrew Junior High School. My friends, the kids in my class, my teachers, the class jerk. *Anyone.*

This was a full-scale disaster. I felt like sirens should be wailing and a SWAT team should be hammering on the door, bellowing through megaphones and swarming down the sides of the duplex.

They weren't.

It was quiet on Dead End Street.

Deathly, deathly quiet.

CHAPTER FOUR

I TRY TO GET YOU ON MY SIDE
EVEN THOUGH I SOUND KIND OF WHINY

I'm calmer now. I've thrown out my *Top Ten Things To Do To Stop Macy* list, which included running away and living in the school Dumpster, blowing up our computer (if baking soda and vinegar do the trick for science-project volcanoes, why wouldn't they work on a hard drive?) and catching a highly contagious, preferably disfiguring disease.

Nothing will work.

Nothing stops Macy. I should know.

So, Spin, you say, trying to be nice even though you're confused and annoyed with me, *what's the big deal? Just tell them you don't want to model anymore. Get out of it. And shut up already.*

Well, I reply, trying to speak slowly and keep my slightly hysterical voice down, *thanks for your understanding and concern, but it's just not that simple.*

Looking at it from your point of view, it must look weird. That's because it *is* weird. Only I didn't realize how weird it was until a few years ago.

It all started when I was six months old. Don't worry: I'm not going to give you a month-by-month summary of my life. Something important happened then.

Now, I know I said "nobody dies" right there in the first chapter of this book. I did not lie about that. But I meant all the people in the story who are currently alive. Living people. The thing is, when I was a baby my dad died in a car accident. It wasn't his fault. It was one of those accidents you read about in the newspapers. Those things actually happen to real, actual people, not just newspaper-headline people. It happened to him. It happened to us.

So maybe what I should have said was, nobody *else* dies. Guaranteed.

Now don't go thinking I'm getting all sad and serious on you here. I'm just explaining. I never knew my dad, although I've heard a lot about him from Mom and Macy. Judging from the stories,

Barry Bryce Spinelli (BB for short, same as old Beauty Boy here) was quite a guy.

"Big BB was so happy! So much fun…" my mom says, her face lighting up.

"A walking teddy bear, God bless him," Macy says. Weird to think that he was her little brother. I look quite a lot like my dad, apparently (although, as I've mentioned already, so does Macy, which is confusing and alarming).

The week after the accident, two things happened: Macy moved in with us to help Mom out, and my baby picture was picked from a ton of other cute-baby pictures sent in by parents (14,213, to be exact) to be on the first cover of *Baby Show* magazine. My dad took the picture. The story goes that he was lying on the floor playing with me, and he snapped a picture of me looking up, amazed, at a bird outside, a perfect drop of drool just falling from my smiling, toothless mouth. He couldn't have known what would happen because of that one picture.

Baby Show started everything.

As a national US magazine, it was huge "exposure" for me, as we say in the business. The Dribbleez Diaper people saw it and contacted my mom about their new diaper campaign. I was the first Dribbleez Cute Patoot! Your parents might even remember me.

Anyway, I was a happy, photogenic baby and the campaign was a big success.

Everything snowballed from there. It's amazing how many companies use babies in their ads. They're like cute, cuddly puppies and kittens, only human. My really fat face was everywhere. And I didn't only appear in ads for baby equipment and baby food. If a car company needed a cute baby for their minivan ad, I was the baby smiling in the car seat. If a flooring company needed a baby to crawl happily across discount carpet, I was that baby. I sold everything. Macy quit her job selling cars and became my full-time agent, selling me.

Mom and Macy threw themselves into my baby-modeling career. It was a whirlwind of bookings and shoots and travel. It became the biggest thing in our lives.

"You saved our lives, BB," Macy once said when I was about ten and we were driving home from a shoot in Red Deer. "Your Mom and me were a total mess after Big BB died. It was so sudden, so senseless." She shook her head, her eyes swimming with tears. "But there you were: beautiful, happy, full of life. Everyone loved you. A little gift from heaven, that's what you were." She reached back and shook my shoulder affectionately. Until it hurt.

The craziness continued into toddlerhood. People love a chubby kid with a dimple and lots of curly dark hair. Especially if you put fake glasses on him! Then he's kind of adorably dorky too!

When I lost my two front teeth, I was solid gold, marketing-wise. Companies love a kid with missing front teeth for some reason. Is it cute or funny or what? I never figured that one out. All I know is that I was working so much I don't even remember kindergarten or grade one.

When I was little, modeling felt normal and (I'm trying to be honest here) even fun. It was exciting to be in modeling shoots and mall fashion shows. I got to go on planes. Everyone told me how cute I was. They smiled and applauded. I felt special and important. It was like playing dress-up every day.

Hey, I was four, okay? Then five and six…

Then it didn't seem so fun. Macy and Mom were so busy and caught up in it that they assumed I was still enjoying it. But I kept noticing more and more that I was different from other kids. I was missing out on things. Other kids went to the movies and played hockey and soccer and went camping and rode their bikes all summer long.

Not me.

Modeling became a grind.

Think of it this way: if every Saturday for your whole life you have broccoli at dinner, you don't even think about it. It's just there, every Saturday, whether you want it or not and whether you like it or not. Pretty soon, broccoli comes to be a part of Saturdays, so you think it's *normal*. You think *everyone* has broccoli on Saturdays.

Then one day, maybe when you're twelve or so, you go over to a friend's house for dinner on Saturday, and they have pizza. And you realize, in a blinding flash, that not everyone has broccoli on Saturdays. It's just your family's version of normal.

(Not a bad little example, hey? For those of you who are wondering what the heck broccoli has to do with anything, broccoli = modeling, and pizza Saturdays = a normal life.)

How have I become almost professional at something I hate doing? It's very complicated, but modeling is really all I know how to do, and I've never had much of a say in it. Macy books the shoots, and I go and pose. End of story. Like I said, it's been happening my whole life. My modeling is also our main source of income. Mom works at a greeting-card store, but other than that, my modeling pays the bills. I don't see much of the money, but I hear I have a killer education fund.

So it's very, very hard to quit. Because it's not just about me. It's about Mom and Macy too. We're all in it. Modeling is still exciting and glamorous to them. They think I'm just one shoot away from a huge contract. They're *proud* of me.

I used to enjoy all the attention that modeling gets you. But I've never enjoyed the actual modeling. Well, once I had a shoot with eight puppies when I was about six years old, and I *loved* that, but that was the *puppies*, not the modeling. Some of the kids I model with, even the normalish ones, really, really *like* it. It matters to them. They talk seriously about their contracts and careers. They *want* their faces on the covers of magazines. They post songs on YouTube, just hoping to be discovered. They dream of big-time runway modeling in places like New York and Paris and Tokyo.

Me? Every shoot, I just want to get out of there. I can barely cope with how things are now, let alone doing *more* modeling, big-time modeling. Contracts? Career? I'm just happy to get some pizza. I'm not looking very far into the future.

But it's getting harder and harder to hide my modeling from everyone else. I lie my head off at school about the days I have to miss for modeling. Sure, Mom calls me in absent, but you have to say something when teachers or your friends ask you why.

I wrote the book on excuses. I've had every cold and flu that's gone around, and even a few tropical diseases. I've been hospitalized several times. I've been to more funerals than is normal for a kid my age. I've had a ton of dental work done, had sick pets and ailing relatives, you name it. Excuses R Us.

Seriously, think about it. Think about what my life would be like if it ever came out that after school and on weekends my main extracurricular activity was *modeling*. Not hockey or gaming or basketball or skateboarding. Modeling.

Yeah, junior-high-school guys would be really supportive and encouraging of that particular career path. Maybe they'd ask to learn a few poses and see my portfolio...or maybe my life would be over. I know for sure that Shay, the loudmouthed jerk in my class, would never, *ever* let me hear the end of it.

Or they might not even believe me, because I'm really just an average-looking guy. Biggish for my age and tending, let's be honest, toward chubbiness. Dark, curly hair, blue eyes. Looking in a mirror, I can see that I'm not an outrageously cute kid anymore. The older I get, the less adorable I become. This has probably been a good thing these last few years. The less adorable, the less in demand, despite Macy's feverish efforts. Maybe I'll have a really ugly adolescence. I can only hope.

Unfortunately, my portfolio makes me look like a movie star. Macy had it done professionally. Some of the photos in there are pretty good. I am photogenic. Some people are, some aren't. Even some really good-looking people aren't photogenic. And some people you wouldn't notice are really photogenic. That's just part of the business.

Of course, my portfolio describes my *ebony curls, classical features and arrestingly deep-blue eyes.* I had nothing to do with that. That's pure Macy.

Portfolios never say *He's just an average, photogenic kid.*

Who would buy that, even if it is the truth?

The problem is Macy. She's determined, this year, to bury me deeper and deeper, until I die of modeling. You have no idea how hard it is to stop Macy when she gets rolling on an idea. The woman is a human tank.

Put yourself in my shoes. Is it so wrong to want to be a normal almost-teenager? To goof around at school with my friends, drink soda, eat pizza and burgers, watch action movies and maybe play hockey (even though I'm no good)? Is it wrong to want to wear sweatpants and *not* have weekly haircuts? Is it wrong to wish a big fuss wasn't made over every pimple or extra pound?

You're thinking I'm being ridiculously dramatic. Am I? *AM I?*

You're sitting there in your smug, non-modeling world shrugging your shoulders, reaching for a piece of pizza and thinking, *So, like I said, quit.*

Like *I* said, it's not that simple.

Look around you. See all those framed photos on the walls of our apartment? Mom and Macy wonder why I never have friends over. Aside from us almost never being home, I mean, look around: there are twelve years of framed photos of me lining the place, like wallpaper.

Twelve years.

My whole life so far. All caught on camera.

→ INTERRUPTION BY MACY #1
(the first of many)

[*There's going to be a bunch of these interruptions in the book. Macy just shouts things out whenever she thinks of them, no matter what you're doing. You're just going to have to put up with them. I have to.*]

"Hey, BEAUTY BOY," Macy called from the computer. I was mid-equation in my math homework at the kitchen table, trying to concentrate. "Now *here's* an interesting one!" She sounded excited. I waited, knowing whatever it was wouldn't interest me even a little bit.

"Awsum Ear Critterz! The company needs 'super-cool teen and preteen models.' Check it out!" She swiveled the computer screen toward me. "Cool earmuff cover thingies in cute designs! Squirrels, frogs, BUNNIES! Aaawww, look!"

Her smile faded as she saw the look on my face.

"Nope. No way, Macy. Those things suck. I hate them."

Okay, I didn't *hate* them. I barely glanced at them, but you have to be blunt with Macy. I've learned this. If I'd tried to be all kind and said, "Yeah, they're sort of cute, but…" I'd have been signed up as chief Critterz model before I knew what was happening.

"I'll take that as a maybe, Mr. Grumpy," she said playfully, turning back to the computer.

See what I mean?

CHAPTER FIVE

FAKE-SKATEBOARDING TO THE OLDIES WITH CHAD AND CODY

I walked into the studio and stopped. I couldn't believe it. Just my luck. I'm in the middle of a crisis, I'm halfway across the country, and out of all the kids I model with, today's shoot is with Chad and Cody.

I know Chad and Cody well. Too well. We've been in tons of shoots together, playing fake football, fake-laughing, fake-shrugging, fake-pointing, etc. We've been fake friends for several years now. Cody's okay. Chad's completely annoying.

"Hey, Cody, hey, Chad," I said with a little sigh.

"Lukester! Dude, wazzzuuuuup?" That was Cody. Cody Radwanski. He's a skinny, goofy redhead with big, super-white teeth and wide, vacant blue eyes.

Remember what I was saying about being photogenic? Well, Cody is. He looks *way* better in pictures than he does in real life. Much cooler too. Pictures don't have audio.

"Hey," said Chad. "We were wondering who the third would be. You're late."

Chad "The Hair" Adams seemed to think I was his competition in his quest to be the World's Top Boy Model. He's a thin little eleven-year-old with a ridiculous swagger, good cheekbones and almost-natural blond hair. His mom's a hairdresser. Oops, sorry: I'm supposed to say "stylist." We almost got into a fight about that once. He's dead serious about modeling and talks about it all the time. Almost as much as he talks about The Hair.

The Hair *always* comes up as a topic of conversation with Chad, like it's an important world event or something. *Breaking news at six: The world financial crisis, war declared and Chad's Hair gets highlighted...*

"Check it out," Chad said, pointing predictably at his head.

"Yeah, man, that is one big head you have there," I murmured. Very witty. It was lost on both of them. Chad always ignored me, and Cody was staring at The Hair, his mouth open, his eyes wide.

Chad patted the spiky tips tenderly with the palm of his hand.

"Highlighted *and* lowlighted," he bragged. "Golden Sunset and Summer Wheat. You'd be looking at three hundred bucks in a salon."

"Coool," breathed Cody, genuinely impressed.

I looked at Cody. He didn't have the natural jerk-o-meter that most people have inside them. The one that shrieks when somebody is lying or bragging or just being a jerk. He took everything at face value. He thought Chad's hair was great because Chad told him it was great. I'm sure he thought we were all good friends. BFFs.

"Okay, boys, let's get at 'er," called Sandra, the photographer. I swung around with relief. Saved from The Hair.

I liked Sandra. She made lame jokes, but she was pretty nice. She actually talked to us about the shoot's "concept," like we were adults.

"So it's basically a summer-skateboard theme," she said.

"Wicked!" murmured Cody, elbowing my arm. *Don't do that, Cody.*

"So what I want," Sandra said, "is action, action, action! Jumps, kicks—you know, skateboard-type stuff. I'm going to shoot you in the air. Action shots. Don't worry about the boards. We'll add them later."

Chad grilled her, professional to professional, about the positioning of the skateboards, the mood, the feel, The Hair, blah, blah, blah.

I stood there with my hands shoved in my board-shorts pockets. The sinking, defeated feeling I got whenever shoots were about to start swept over me.

Cody nudged me hard, his face lighting up with excitement.

"Let's do this thannng!!" he yelled, even though I was only six inches away. *Don't do that, Cody.*

"I am *sooo* going to ollie," he grinned, pumping his fist in the air. I was very sure he didn't have a clue what an ollie was. He was one of those guys who wears skateboard gear and talks a lot but is fundamentally unathletic. And did I mention uncool?

I looked at Cody's vacant, excited face and wondered if life might be easier without much of a brain.

We moved to the "set"—some bright lights against a sky-blue backdrop.

Sandra pushed a large button on the ancient boom box that she carted to shoots. Some really lame nineties music blared out for our supercool, awesomely rad, action-packed, oldies' boarding party.

Okay, get up. Put the book down for a minute. If I gotta do this, so do you.

Forget about your fake-skateboard. Stand with your knees bent, arms raised and action-posed, then hop into the air and pretend you're doing tricks. Swivel your hips, bend your legs like you've just kickflipped the board behind you; improvise. And smile like you're having the time of your life while you're doing it. Like you're *exhilarated*. Keep smiling and hopping idiotically for at least half an hour.

Cody actually, really, truly looked like he was having the time of his life. Maybe he was. How sad is that?

"Can't touch this!" he screamed with the music as he flailed away beside me.

Chad was more controlled. A serious 'boarder dude, doing serious 'boarder moves. He always stared straight at the camera with a smoldering, direct look.

Chad's already paranoid about his "good side." Apparently it's his left, the one with the dimple. He jockeys around during every shoot so that his left side is to the camera. Once he gets there, he relaxes and lets the dimple do its magic.

Chad also mutters "Click it" under his breath continually, like he's telling the photographer what to do. It doesn't mean anything. It's just a phrase he repeats *over and over* when he's modeling. I find it unbelievably annoying.

I did my best, hopping and grunting to the oldies. I knew Macy had worked hard to get me this shoot, and I knew it paid a lot.

"And UP and FUN...kicking...big smiles and JUMP...woo-hoo, that's it, that...is...IT!" Sandra kept up a running commentary as she crouched and shot. Cody kept slamming into me, forcing me into Chad, who elbowed me hard whenever he had the chance. *Stuck in the Middle: The Luke Spinelli Story*.

Sandra stopped when we were getting hot and red. In advertising, nobody sweats.

Oh, if you're still jumping and fake-skateboarding like a fool, you can stop now too.

Five-minute break.

CHAPTER SIX

SHAY, THE ART OF BULLYING AND AGLETS

Bullies.

Most books and shows, in my opinion, get them all wrong. They're usually just totally unrealistic. Beefy, sadistic captain-of-the-football-team jocks who live only to slam impossibly nerdy kids into lockers or toilets. Muscle-bound freaks stealing skinny kids' lunch money. Always big, always vicious.

In my experience, though, the big bullying jerks account for only a small percentage of actual bullies these days. Maybe 5 or 10 percent. In fact, I can think of only one in my school: Tyson Kemp, a kid who is *way* bigger and more freakishly energetic than everyone else.

Tyson is the reason my junior high went through this hypervigilant anti-bullying campaign. We now have a zero-tolerance policy on violence.

That sounds good, and it does limit kids like me getting beaten up. And Tyson is out of business and now has to sit still, quietly growing his facial hair and not understanding math ever.

But the anti-bullying policy also means no snowball-throwing or tackle football. I even got hauled to the office last semester for arm-wrestling at lunch. Ryan Shewchuk got suspended for throwing a piece of ice against the Dumpster. The *Dumpster*. Can you even bully a Dumpster?

Anyway, in my school, the days of the big, burly bullies are over. But a new, even more vicious species of bully has taken their place: the mind-bullies. Way meaner. Way, way more dangerous.

Take Shay, a guy in my class. I know, I know: what kind of name is that? I've asked myself that too, and I don't know. Irish? I've never asked him. You wouldn't either.

Shay's not your stereotypical bully. He's puny—probably under five feet tall—wiry and skinny. Sounds completely harmless, right? Wrong. Shay is smart, cunning and absolutely ruthless. He's kind of a combination bully-jerk. A burk.

Last week, Shay convinced a substitute teacher that he was a hearing-impaired student. That poor woman yelled her way through our math class, gulping water like crazy while we all killed ourselves laughing behind our books. Shay sat there poker-faced, sort of tilting his right ear toward her and saying loudly, "I'm sorry, I didn't get that." He gets away with these kinds of things.

When he gets bored, he looks for evil ways to brighten his life. Like, he'll call across the room to a shy, quiet girl named Madison and say, "Madison, that's enough! Shut up already! You talk WAY too much." She'll get a really red face and stare down at her desk. And he'll keep it up, turning around and shushing her all period. It's stupid stuff, I know, but he always gets everyone to look. It's even worse when he gets everyone to laugh.

He gets sent to the office all the time. I don't know if our teacher, Ms. McCoy, just wants to get rid of him for a while or really sees it as a punishment. He loves it. He'll even suggest it. "Ms. McCoy, I really think I should be sent to the office." She hates that, but she's trapped. She needs him gone so we can get some real work done. I don't envy her at all.

Shay is a kind of roving bully. This is really a stroke of genius, bully-wise, because everyone knows they could be a potential victim. You never know when he's going to pick on you. Today I was the target. It started early: 8:25 AM.

"Well, well, Mr. Spinelli," Shay called out as I walked into class, "good of you to *finally* join us." I had missed a couple of days for the shoot with Chad and Cody.

"Um, good to be here," I mumbled.

Part of the problem is that I can never think up smart things to say. Shay always makes me feel dumb and slow and clumsy.

He was standing over near Edie's desk, pestering a group of girls. Edie's got long brown hair and brown eyes, and she draws on her jeans. She's very cool without trying to be. Edie's probably the only one in the class who talks back to Shay, who doesn't care what he does. This, of course, drives him crazy.

"You've missed two days, Spin. Again. These absences are starting to look suspicious. Where have you been?" he asked.

All the girls looked over at me expectantly. All of them but Edie, who was drawing on her binder. She draws really well. Mostly dragons and wizards and castles, with bolts of lightning.

My mind went blank. I froze, forgetting which excuse I had used last time. Usually I rehearse on the way to school which excuse I'm going to use. I should really write them all down, and note the days I've used them. Sort of an excuses catalog. You can only have so many grandparents' funerals to attend until someone does the math. I frantically searched my mind for all the other relatives I'd invented in my large, imaginary Italian family.

Edie looked up at Shay and said in her slow, bored way, "What're you, his *mom*?"

Everyone laughed. I laughed too and said, "Yeah, good of you to care, Shay." I edged away, over to my desk. Shay looked murderous. I'd pay for this.

What're you, his mom? It was the perfect retort. Why couldn't I ever think of things like that? I would have stammered out some kind of excuse, as if I *owed* it to Shay to tell him where I'd been. Or, more accurately, to lie about where I'd been.

Imagine, just imagine, if I'd said, "Well, Shay, as a matter of fact, I was doing fake ollies and kickflips with a couple of other boy models." My life would have been *over*.

Shay watched me as I wandered over to Chan and Frey.

Oops, sorry—you haven't met them yet. The little guy with glasses is Daniel Chan, and the big, sloppy guy with the food stains on his clothes is Andrew Frey.

But I never call them Daniel and Andrew, or even Dan and Andy. We've been one-syllable-last-name friends for years.

"Spin!" said Chan. "Can you *tell* this guy"—he gestured to Frey—"what that little thing at the end of your shoelace is? *Tell* him."

"It's an aglet," I answered.

"See? Frey, see? I told you it had a name." Chan is an excitable guy. A details guy.

"I didn't say it didn't have a name," said Frey slowly. Everything about Frey is slow. He talks slowly. He blinks slowly. He shuffles slowly. His three brothers are the same, only in varying sizes of huge. Right now, Frey was slowly tying his shoelace. Both aglets, incidentally, had burst or fallen off, so the ends were fuzzy and frayed. Aglet-less.

"I said I didn't care," he said finally.

Hard to argue with that. That's what I like about Chan and Frey. They never ask where I've been or what I've been doing. They just talk to me like I've been there the whole time. This stupid conversation about shoelaces was comforting, somehow.

As I slid into my desk, I looked over at Shay. He was still staring at me, his eyes narrowed. I hate it when that happens.

I'd rather people didn't look.

→ INTERRUPTION BY MACY #2

"Oho, BEAUTY BOY! Here we go," called Macy from the computer. "Slinkee Jeans is looking for 'rebels and rockers' for its revolutionary new 'Teen Jean Scream campaign!' Sounds pretty radical, hey?"

Radical? Is it 1985?

You know me pretty well by now. Would you describe me as a rebel? A rocker? A revolutionary? Me neither. Can you imagine me in anything called Slinkee Jeans? They sound tight. If they want a kid looking pained, awkward and uncomfortable, I'm their guy.

"Ehhhhnnngh," I said loudly, like someone hitting the Wrong Answer button. "No way."

"I think we need some more information on this one, cranky-pants," Macy murmured, typing.

I lowered my head to the table, banging it softly.

CHAPTER SEVEN

LEADING US INTO (ONE OF) MY BIGGEST LIES EVER

Macy's steamrolling ahead now, booking more and more modeling gigs. It's every weekend now, some weekdays, even a few evenings. All part of her master plan to completely ruin my life.

Well, I'm thinking there can be two master plans.

Old Spin might have a few surprises up his size-twelve sleeve.

"You'll have to miss some school, honey. Quite a lot of school," my mom said, looking worried. She was staring at all the bookings on The Calendar That Rules Our Lives. I hate that calendar. It doesn't even have any pictures. Just huge squares and red ink.

"Busy month coming up," she said.

I always do well in school, so missing some days has never seemed to be a big problem. But grown-ups are supposed to worry about kids missing school. Not Macy. For Macy, the modeling always comes first. I think Macy sees it as our ticket to the big time, to the huge contract that is always just around the corner.

But Mom is different. With Mom, school comes first. She actually reads my report cards, even all those cut-and-paste sentences that every kid in the class gets. This was a good time to complain a little. And exaggerate.

"You know, Mom, I'm finding it hard to keep up, missing so much school," I said, looking up from watching highlights of the Flames–Canucks game. It wasn't true though. Chan took great notes, and I studied when I was on the road. I like school. I hate missing classes.

"Really? That's not good. I had no idea. Look, I'll talk to Macy, okay?"

Excellent. Macy listens to Mom. Mom is about two feet shorter and a lot quieter, but she's tough too. She's had to be, to put up with Macy for all these years. There was nothing much she could do about the dates that had been booked, but maybe she could sort of slow Macy down.

"Hey," she said, looking over at me. "Everything else okay?"

Here was my chance. My chance to complain, whine and rant about Macy ruining my life. I opened my mouth. It was hard to know where to start.

"Well, you know, Mom, lately…"

The front doorbell rang, long and loud. Macy. She had a key but never seemed to use it. She just rang whenever she needed to get in. She came in fuming about some appointment she'd had, and the conversation that Mom and I were about to have never happened.

After dinner, Mom knocked on my door. She was shrugging into her coat. Mom is always rushing somewhere. She takes evening classes at a community college toward a diploma in business management and administration. I'm proud of her for going to school while she works full-time. Other than being freakishly busy all the time, she seems to like it.

I, on the other hand, clearly have no future in business, because all her courses sound stupefyingly boring. Beyond boring. Deathly. "Corporate Structure and Governance," "Statistics and Quality Assurance," that sort of thing. Blah-blah and blah-blah. Just the words make my brain turn off. They make my science unit on "The Structure and Organization of the Plant Kingdom" sound wildly exciting.

"I know it's not *scintillating*," she said once, "but it's important. I'm actually becoming qualified for something other than reorganizing the sympathy-card section. I'll get a better job, a *career*..." She had big plans.

She stood in the doorway, winding a scarf around her neck.

"BB, I have to get to class, but I will have that talk with Macy. She's booking too much during school."

"Yep, couldn't agree more, Mom."

"But we do need to let the school know why you'll be gone so much," she said firmly. She knew I wanted to keep the modeling a secret, but she didn't approve of lying.

"Look," she said. "Your principal will probably be totally impressed! Ever thought of that?"

For a smart person, my mom could be completely clueless. It wasn't about anyone being impressed or not; it was about making sure I could survive junior high. She just didn't understand that lying had become totally, utterly necessary. If I told Mrs. Walker, how could I trust her not to tell anyone else? How could I ever be sure? I'd live in fear and dread that the secret would get out.

"Look, Mom," I said, "you'd better write me a note. Just something *vague*, about me missing school.

I'll *talk* to Mrs. Walker and let her know why. Leave it to me."

She looked at me hard. The woman is no fool.

"Nothing in writing, hey? Okay, listen, Luke, if I write you a general note, you *promise* me you'll tell Mrs. Walker the details?"

"Yeah, sure," I said. Lie.

"So I can trust you on this?" she continued.

"You can trust me," I lied confidently. I'm such a jerk.

She smiled, then glanced at her watch.

"Yikes, I'm late. Okay, general note…" She sat down at my desk, grabbed a piece of loose-leaf and wrote.

"Done. Got to go. Love you." She kissed the top of my head and left.

I read the note. It said:

Dear Mrs. Walker,

My son, Luke Spinelli, will have to be absent for quite a few days in the next little while. I will let him explain to you why he'll be absent, and we would like that reason to be kept <u>private</u>. He will keep up with his schoolwork, so please let his teachers know.

Thank you for your understanding,
Kathy Spinelli

This was good. Nice and vague. Now all I had to do was come up with a reason.

A reason that was way, *way* different than the truth.

A reason that was believable, but didn't lead to much investigation.

A reason that was a question-stopper.

It was going to be a lie. That wasn't an issue. The issue was how big a lie I was comfortable with.

Pretty big, as it turns out.

* * *

An hour later I was still at my desk, gnawing on the end of my pencil. (Everyone tells me that's a disgusting habit. It probably is, but that doesn't seem to stop me from having to floss orange pencil paint out of my teeth.)

Anyway, this was significant gnawing. Important gnawing. I had to invent a disease. Ever invented a disease? Not an easy thing. The thing is, when you think *disease*, you think of all the ones you know. All the ones you've heard of.

Here's the problem. I knew I was a jerk for going behind my mom's back, inventing a disease and planning to tell the principal it's the reason I have to miss school. But somehow, I wasn't quite such a jerk that I was going to use an actual disease that actual people are suffering from. Even jerks have a code they live by. A jerk code of honor. And, bizarrely, it appears that lying about having an actual disease is against my jerk's code of honor. Who knew?

So what I needed was a completely new, very serious, totally made-up disease. This was a very tricky thing to do. It had to *sound* legit but in reality be *not legit*. Believable, but a complete lie…

So I gnawed. I have to tell you, I was coming up with nothing but blanks. *Think illness, think disease…* I tried body parts, but that just got ridiculous. I mean, who was going to believe I had Multiplestomachosity?

I got out my dictionary. There was a chart of some bits of words that go before and after a real word to make it sound more Latin-y. I've noticed many illnesses have a Latin-like name. Or Greek, probably, but I only had the Latin.

I needed a main part to attach the Latin-y bits to. The main part of the illness.

*Think, Spin, think…*I looked around my room. My eyes fell on the games stacked on my shelves. The ones we never seemed to have time to play. Hmmm…

After scribbling and scratching out such obviously lame fake diseases as Battleshiposity and SupraClue Trauma, I hit on Cranium. Cranium…Cranium*ectomy*! I started to get excited. That sounded super Latiny.

That is, until I figured out that it meant "surgical removal of the brain." Not, maybe, exactly what I was looking for.

Scrabble, Candyland...wait, *Candyland*? What am I, four years old? Mental note: clean room.

And then, there it was. The game I was sure I could work into a disease. Monopoly. Only I'd change the spelling a bit—Monopoli—and add a suffix. Monopoli*osis*? Monopoli*itis*? I kind of liked the cool double *ii* of the last one.

Now, to do a lie properly, you have to sell it. If I went in there whining "I have MONOPOLYitis," Mrs. Walker would obviously just think I was some kid who'd made up a disease out of the board game. Am I right?

That's why you pronounce it "mono-poli-itis". Emphasis on all three parts, see? And you say it seriously, while looking the person in the eye. And maybe you gesture to your chest or something.

I heard the front door slam. I opened my door a crack and peeked out. I was in luck. Macy, the house computer hog, was outside "stretching her legs" (which I knew really meant having a quick cigarette out by the Dumpster).

I hurried over to the computer. I felt like one of those heroes in action movies who have to type really quickly because they're doing something they shouldn't be, maybe trying to hack into a bad guy's computer while he's coming down the hall...

But I had to be sure. The jerk code book was telling me I had to be sure.

I googled M-o-n-o-p-o-l-i-i-t-i-s.

Ka-ching!

No matches. Not one.

Entirely made up.

What do you know? I think I have my disease.

CHAPTER EIGHT

I UNLEASH THE MONSTER LIE

"Yeah, most people haven't heard of it," I said, staring Mrs. Walker straight in the eye. "It's a rare disease, but serious." I closed my eyes for a second, as if feeling the pain. "But we're really hoping the operation might help."

The principal stared at me. So long that I began to wonder if I was as good a liar as I thought. My heart began to thud loudly.

Finally, she sighed.

"I'm so sorry, Luke. This all sounds like quite an ordeal for you."

I nodded bravely.

"Yep, so that's why I have to miss those big chunks of school. Surgery. Recovery. Uh, therapy. Mom is so upset she can't talk about it. She just can't. Really, don't talk to her about it. At all."

"Of course, of course," Mrs. Walker murmured, wiping her eyes behind her thick glasses. "I'm sorry, but I hate to think of you, a *child*, going though such pain."

Okay, I have to admit that when she started crying, I felt totally horrible. I thought she'd be kind of businesslike about it—ask for doctor's notes and stuff like that. I just about caved when those tears welled up.

I should have remembered that Mrs. Walker is emotional. She tells kids who get sent to the office all the time, like Shay, that she *believes* in them. She puts together these inspirational, be-all-you-can-be PowerPoint presentations for our assemblies, sets them to very lame, sappy music, and sits and tears up at how wonderful we all are.

She's a good person. And it sucks lying to good people. I could lie to mean, stupid people all day long, but the nice ones make a good lie almost impossible.

I sat there feeling miserable, and not just because of the fake disease. There was nothing I could do now. I mean, I couldn't all of a sudden say, "Just kidding!"

She asked me a few gentle questions, like "Are you in pain?" and "What's the prognosis?"

Hmmm, if I knew what that word meant, I might be able to answer you, I thought. I just shook my head sadly. That seemed to do the trick.

"I really don't want anyone to know, Mrs. Walker," I pleaded. "Can you just tell my teachers I'm a little sick or something? Everything is…hard enough already," I choked out.

Okay, I know what you're thinking: *This guy is a complete and total JERK*! Well, I guess there might be some other jerk out there thinking, *You go, Spin*! Anyway, I felt like a real jerk. Worse than a jerk.

But believe me, I'd used up every single other halfway-believable excuse. Every one. I told you that a few chapters ago. In the lying business, you have to keep things fresh. It'd be insulting otherwise. I'm not a my-dog-ate-my-homework kind of liar. I'm an artist.

There was a long, awkward silence. I didn't feel right about breaking it. I mean, you don't drop a depressing bombshell and then jump up, check your watch and say, "Well, lunchtime, gotta go!"

Finally, Mrs. Walker got up and held out her hand. Her face was all blotchy, and her hand was really warm.

"Luke, I'm honored that you chose to tell me about your illness. And I want you to know that this school, this *family*, will stand behind you one hundred percent. A *thousand* percent," she said. (Chan hates stuff like that. I can just see him putting his big head to the side, narrowing his eyes and snapping, "There's no such *thing* as a thousand percent." Good thing Chan'll never know that he and the "family" are that much behind me.)

I looked at the door behind Mrs. Walker and thought, *Please don't hug me please don't hug me please don't hug me…*

The phone rang.

I can move quickly when I need to. I shook Mrs. Walker's hand up and down a few times, muttered "thanks" and bolted for the door.

Even a jerk gets lucky once in a while.

CHAPTER NINE

RED PLUSH (A PLACE. NOT, THANKFULLY, AN OUTFIT I HAVE TO MODEL)

Today was going to be the last day for a while that I had free time after school. I needed it. Mrs. Walker had popped by our class after lunch "Just to say hi!" and given me a brave, supportive smile. She'd also left an inspirational quotation on my locker (which I ripped off and crumpled up as soon as I saw it). It said: *Bravery is the smile worn by a trembling soul.* What the heck? Why should something I didn't even understand make me feel like garbage?

It was nice to hang out with Chan and Frey for a while. They're total goofs, and we laugh a lot. Not fake-laughing either. Actual friends having actual, unphotogenic good times.

We headed over to Red Plush, a movie-rental store about three blocks from our school, tucked in the dark end of a grim little strip mall. I can't figure out how it stays in business, because there never seems to be anyone in there but us. We pushed open the door that still, at 3:30 PM, had the CLOSED sign on it.

"Uh-oh, look out. Here comes trouble," rasped a voice as the little bells above the door jangled.

Red (none of us knew her last name) said the same thing every time we came in. She was a tiny, shriveled old woman with patchy, dyed-red hair and big, watery, blue eyes. She mostly sat in a recliner with her veiny legs up, watching old movies.

She turned toward us, smiling.

Now, if you didn't know Red, that smile might have made you turn and run.

First, her teeth were not terrific. With modern advances in dental care, most people don't have *black* teeth anymore. But Red had a few, and you could see them all when she smiled. Second, there was, as Chan called it, her "extreme makeup." We'd had arguments, just us three, about whether she used markers or crayons or small paintbrushes.

Whatever she used, the effect was very dramatic. Okay, I'm being diplomatic. She looked completely creepy, like an old-lady zombie or maybe like a little

girl who got turned into a creepy old-lady zombie.
I'm not really putting this well.

Today's look was bright orange lipstick WAY outside
the lines, bright blue eye shadow sweeping around her
eyes and up the sides of her bony forehead, and two
blotches of pink on her withered cheeks.

Anyway, no matter what she looked like, Red was
super nice. Like a grandmother who never tried to
kiss you or told you to cut your hair or tucked your
shirt in for you at the back of your pants. Red pretty
much just offered you snacks and left you alone.

"Hey, Red," Frey called out cheerfully. "How's
business?" Frey lives down the street, so he and Red
know each other pretty well. Frey shovels the walks
at Red Plush when it snows, runs (or sort of shuffles)
errands for her and helps (slowly) with any lifting.

"Oh, okay. Steady," she replied, her eyes wandering
back to the black-and-white movie on the ancient TV.

I noticed the cover was still on the cash register.
How does this place stay in business? I wondered for the
millionth time. Humphrey, Red's slobbery bulldog,
slid off the couch and snuffled over to us. I bent down
and gave his ears a good scratch. He loves that.

I love dogs. Dogs don't know when you're lying
or what kind of problems you have. They don't care.
They just like you (or not), and they show it. Often
with drool.

"You boys want some popcorn? Or there's cookies." Red waved her blue-veiny hand toward the back of the store.

Frey, always hungry, was already rummaging. With four boys, the Frey household is always short on food. I've known Frey to bring nothing but two whole carrots, with the green tops still on, for lunch. He will sit there, chewing like a barnyard animal, totally oblivious to any snickers from me and Chan. Actually, Frey often eats most of Chan's lunch as well. Mrs. Chan packs Chan these mammoth lunches—spring rolls, rice, noodles, stir-fried vegetables and pork. They're the best lunches in the class. Ask anyone.

Chan and I tucked our backpacks out of the way and sat on the couch. Red Plush was kind of a run-down place, but it was a neat idea. The main room was set up like a living room: a couch and Red's recliner faced a TV hooked up to an old VCR and a newer DVD player. And along the wall, bolted to the floor, there was this cool row of old, red, velvety movie seats. Red got them from some theater that was demolished. Anyway, the movies were like an afterthought, lining the rest of the walls in crooked, haphazard bunches.

In most movie-rental stores, the movies are organized into sections. Drama, comedy, family, classics... that kind of thing. At Red Plush, it was all random, and you pretty much had to ask Red where anything was. Sometimes we'd quiz her just to keep her on her toes.

"*Sunset Boulevard*," Chan would say.

"Easy. Second from the bottom of that pile near the till. Watched it yesterday."

"*Aladdin.*" There didn't seem to be anything newer than about 1980 in the store, except the Disney movies. She seemed to have a soft spot for those.

"Top shelf by the door," she'd rattle off. "Fourth from the left."

"Ah, but do you know where *The Troll Diaries* is?" Chan would slip in.

Red would turn, wagging her finger, giving him the full benefit of her terrible face.

"You little rat, Chan, you're making them up again. Whaddaya think I am, an amateur?"

I had to hand it to her: she knew her stuff.

Red Plush was very comfortable, especially on winter afternoons. Most days, Red had a portable heater going full blast along with the central heating, so the place was very cozy, especially if you'd trudged there through three feet of snow in runners and a hoodie. Nobody in grade seven wears snow boots. Ever.

Anyway, it was a great place. I hadn't told Mom or Macy about it. Another secret, but can you blame me? It was a quiet place, a place to watch an ancient

John Wayne western, eat popcorn and forget that, instead of saving the good townsfolk from vicious cattle-rustling thugs, you had to go model cheap clothes on the weekend.

I wondered what the Duke (that's what they used to call John Wayne) would have said about it.

On second thought, I didn't want to know.

→ INTERRUPTION BY MACY #3

"Now, Beauty Boy, just listen to this one. Just *listen*: 'Warmer-Weave Undershirts needs teen models with spark and sass for its *We Want U* campaign.'" She looked up hopefully.

I have to hand it to Macy. She just keeps on trying.

Hmmm, let me think. A semi-naked modeling shoot...

"Listen, Macy, absolutely not. ABSOLUTELY NEVER," I said menacingly. It bounced right off her.

She actually laughed.

"You look so funny when you're trying to be Mr. Tough Guy, BB! *Absolutely never!*" she mimicked in a stupid, exaggerated growl. "Well, we'll see, BB. We shall see. But you know what they say? Never say never!" she said playfully, taking a sip of her coffee and swiveling back to the computer.

CHAPTER TEN

ANOTHER SUPER-EXCITING SHOOT WITH SUPER-JOCK CODY

Toronto. I know nothing about the city, other than Pearson Airport (which is just like other airports, only bigger) and the insides of budget motels and photo studios. We drove past the CN Tower once, but that was about it for sightseeing. We come here, I model, we leave.

Cody and I were standing by the water cooler, on a break from grinning and shrugging. The waistband of my pants was killing me, digging a red, itchy line across my stomach.

"They told me you were a size twelve!" the assistant snapped when I mentioned how tight it was.

"Well, sometimes I take a twelve, sometimes a fourteen," I explained patiently. In my head, I was ranting:

*Listen, you hag, I can barely breathe in these things...
you try wearing pants seventy sizes too small...see how
you like it...*

"Well, suck in your gut, because that's the outfit for
the shoot. I've only got the one size."

What a charmer, hey? I also distinctly heard her
muttering something about me "laying off the pizza"
as she walked away. There's nothing you can do with
people like that. Either you burst a blood vessel or
you let it go. I shrugged, a real, philosophical shrug.
Not the fake kind we were doing in the shoot.

Anyway, me and Cody were standing by the water
cooler. Cody and I. Whatever. I was running a finger
under my waistband, wondering how much longer we
needed to be there. Cody was talking.

"Pretty sweet shoot, hey, Lukester?" he asked. He
really meant it. He was having *fun* at this lame-o
shoot. The brilliant idea of the whole thing was that
we were these cute kids who accidentally hit a baseball
through a fake broken window. Oops! I never understand why companies think this kind of thing will sell
clothes. Anyway, I tried to tell the photographer that
it wasn't very believable that I'd be holding a bat and
wearing a ball glove as well. I mean, you either bat or
field in baseball, right?

"Well, we're just trying to get across the *idea* of
baseball, Luke. Just, you know, *baseball*. The ball in

the window. Nobody's thinking of the *rules*," laughed the photographer.

So there I stood, stupidly wearing a ball mitt while holding the bat, and trying to look like I didn't mind.

We had just finished a series of shots where we were supposed to "shrug endearingly" (about fake-breaking the window) while looking straight into the camera.

Try it: put your hands deep in your pockets, kind of straighten your arms, hunch up your shoulders near your ears, furrow your brow and smile kind of ruefully.

If you're super corny, like Cody, you might turn in your toes, or even push out your bottom lip. Photographers love that kind of stuff. That's why Cody will go far in this business. He understands it. He *believes* in it.

I felt kind of sorry for him.

"Yep, it's a riot, Cody," I said.

Cody got serious all of a sudden.

"Marnie's leaving," he said, looking like he was going to cry. Cody always assumed you knew who he was talking about. He's the kind of guy who would get on a city bus, sit right behind the driver, blurt "Marnie's leaving" and never once think, *Oh, wait, this guy's a total stranger who might not know Marnie or care about why she's leaving.*

"Oh yeah?" I said. "That sucks. Who's Marnie again?"

"Marnie? Oh, Grams," he said, surprised. "You know, Grams. My agent?"

Aaaah, the old lady Cody always came with. She was about a hundred and fifty. Grams. Maybe that was why I thought she was his grandma. Actually, I thought she was his *great*-grandma. I guess she's his agent—or was his agent.

"Oh yeah, yeah, her," I said quickly. "Where's she going?"

"Florida. Forever," he said, sounding lost.

"Hey, no snow shoveling there," I said, trying to lighten things up. "Try and set up a visit every February, Cody. Work on the tan."

His big eyes brimmed with tears.

I rattled on nervously.

"Seriously, there are other agents, Cody. You're really good. You won't have any trouble finding another agent. They'll be lining up…"

I was talking quickly. We were on again in about five seconds. I could see the photographer and the props guy chucking their Styrofoam coffee cups in the garbage. Ever heard of the *environment*, you jerks?

I turned back to Cody, hoping he wasn't bawling now. And then a light went on in my brain.

"Hey, Cody, you should talk to my Aunt Macy. She's my agent, and she's really good. She's started a modeling agency, and I know she's looking for some new clients."

He brightened immediately, like babies do when you shake some keys in front of them. Shiny! Noisy!

"Thanks, Luke," he said. "Macy even *sounds* like Marnie. I'm gonna do it! You're a good friend. A really good friend."

Awkward man-hug alert! I stepped back just as Cody stepped toward me, so he kind of punched my shoulder instead, which was way, *way* better. I lightly punched him back, feeling guilty for all the times I got frustrated with Cody, said mean things about him in my mind and felt like he was a loser. He wasn't a bad guy. Just kind of goofy and vacant. There I go again. He's a good guy. Period.

"BOYS?" bellowed the photographer.

"Time to rock and roll, Lukester!" Cody whispered, his face lighting up.

CHAPTER ELEVEN

NORMAL-ISH BOY MODEL SEEKS HOCKEY TEAM

I'm a big hockey fan. As big a fan as you can be when you can't play on a team or watch almost any NHL games. But I always know who's playing, I check the scores, and I cheer to myself.

Chan and Frey play hockey in a league. As far as I can figure it out, this is how leagues work: the guys who've been in skates since they were sucking on a soother play in the A league, with the burly coaches who act as if their players are almost semiprofessional.

The A-league guys all wait by the phone for the NHL to call them up. The parents are, shall we say, very, *very* involved. I once saw Ethan Malloy's dad scream so hard that he horked a gob of spit onto the Plexiglas two rows down. I watched that spit trickle down into the boards the whole third period. Not pretty. My mom would say Mr. Malloy has issues.

Chan and Frey play on the same team, in the D or F league, meaning they can stand up on skates and have parents that don't mind driving them to early Saturday-morning practices.

It's my kind of league. Nobody scores much, but they have fun. Chan's actually really fast, in an out-of-control kind of way. It's the stopping he has trouble with. He generally just skids into the boards and falls, crashing into a crumpled heap. Frey plays defense. BIG defense. He doesn't move much, but he doesn't have to. His skill is being almost impossible to get around.

I really thought this would be the year I got to play, but you-know-what got in the way.

"Hmmm. Hockey, hey?" Mom said, looking over the registration forms. I'd sneakily made sure Macy was out before I showed Mom the forms.

"Yeah, I got it all figured out," I said quickly. "I get Frey to lend me some secondhand equipment. The Frey guys all play hockey. There's got to be some old gear lying around."

I thought I had her, I really did. Then she flipped through the pages of The Calendar That Rules Our Lives.

Have I mentioned that I hate that calendar? I think I did.

It's always booked solid, the dates of modeling shoots in red. I looked over at it. There was a lot of red.

"Oh, honey, I'm sorry, but it looks like in the fall you're booked every Saturday until Christmas," she said. "I guess that's the price you pay for being gorgeous! Maybe next year, okay?"

"Okay," I said, trying to smile back at her.

Now, when I was younger I would have just shrugged this off as another thing in a long list of things I couldn't do, like eating donuts, cutting my own hair and using non-whitening toothpaste.

But I'm twelve now. And I'm getting angry. Slow-burn Spin, that's me. Man on the edge.

Anyway, I go and watch Chan crash and Frey be immobile when I can. And we play after school sometimes with Frey's brothers at the park near Frey's house. It's just a little field in the summer, with an old climber and two baby swings in one corner. But in the winter, Frey's dad puts up some two-by-fours and floods the field every night for a week as soon as we get a cold snap.

It's like the Frey family's personal rink. Their two nets stay on the ice, and the boys and their friends do all the shoveling. One of the only rules is, you want to play, you have to shovel. When you finish playing, you just dump all your goalie pads and sticks and helmets in a heap at one end of the rink, knowing that another group of kids will be out playing soon.

More than once, I've strapped on goalie stuff that was frozen solid, like big blocks of ice. The equipment is not exactly state-of-the-art gear: helmets with flapping grills held on by a single, ancient screw, gloves with holes in the leather. No A-league guy would touch it, but hey, I'll take it.

Some of my best memories are from that park, playing out there with frozen hands until I couldn't even see the puck. Then, when it was hopelessly dark, some Frey would shout, "ARE...YOU...READY... FOR...EXTREME HOCKEY?" which is just skating wildly and crashing into each other randomly in the dark. It's awesome.

Last year, Nick (Frey's oldest brother) decided to ask his dad to put in floodlights.

"Yeah, and a hot-chocolate machine," chipped in Chan, blowing on his hands.

"Benches!" said Frey, brushing snow off his enormous backside.

"How about bleachers for all our fans?" I suggested, gesturing to two elderly ladies at a bus stop across the field.

None of it happened. But we still have the old equipment, the goals and EXTREME HOCKEY.

But listen up, sports fans: Big News!

Now, for the first time in my life, I might have a chance to be on a *real* hockey team. My school is putting together a team for a citywide junior-high tournament.

Chan told me about it at lunch.

"So it's a few weeks of practices and one tournament," he said, pushing up his glasses. "And here's the best thing, Spin. All the guys who really play hockey have provincials that weekend, so they're not trying out. Mr. Schulz said to get the word out that we really need bodies!"

They need bodies! *Bodies!* I'm a body! This was my kind of team.

I peppered him with questions.

"Any early-morning practices?" This would be a deal breaker for Mom and Macy.

"There are two, but my dad says we can pick you up," said Chan.

I gnawed on my thumbnail. Where was a pencil when I needed one? I could already hear the crowd chanting, *Go, Spin, go!*

"Chan, you know I'm not very good. You've seen me play. Not so good with the turning and the stopping. Or the puck handling or the shooting. Do you think I'd make it?" I asked.

"Geez, Spin, have you been listening?" He spoke slowly. "We…need…bodies. To fill positions. So we can play. Get it? Just show up."

"Yeah, just shut up and show up, Spin," said Frey through a mouthful of my celery sticks.

So I did. I showed up.

And I made the team. I made it!

Sure, *everyone* who showed up made the team.

Sure, my number 13 jersey is faded orange and reeks of years of other guys' sweat.

Sure, I still have to find some equipment so I don't actually die out there.

Sure, I still have to break it to Mom and Macy, which won't be pretty.

But I'm on a *hockey team*. Playing real hockey. Real shots, real skating.

Ice, Stick and Puck: The Luke Spinelli Story.

CHAPTER TWELVE

A NOTE FROM THE EDITOR

In this chapter, Mr. Spinelli attempted, unsuccessfully, to describe a "gruesome" Valentine's Day–themed modeling shoot with Clarissa, "Psycho-Freak Girl Model," during which they were required to freeze a "pucker-pose."

In another pose, they were "forced to hold hands and fake-skip together."

Due to the extreme distaste (to say nothing of the inappropriate language) our author showed for describing this shoot, it has been omitted.

He requests that we remind you that he promised to be honest.

He did not promise to tell you everything.

Please respect his privacy in this deeply painful matter.

CHAPTER THIRTEEN

IN WHICH MY MONSTER LIE GROWS AND LURCHES OUT OF CONTROL

I'm back. If you have any questions about that last chapter, keep them to yourselves.

Remember: I'm a man on the edge. Things could blow up any chapter here. Like, for example, in this one.

First thing this morning, Mrs. Walker came on the intercom, all serious and solemn.

"Students and staff," she began, "I would like to take this opportunity to announce that our junior-high community will be promoting a new initiative…"

Do all principals talk like that? All "initiative" this and "strategy" that and blah, blah, blah? I was barely listening. I was busy with my ongoing project of using my Sharpie to turn my blue binder completely black.

"…committed to social justice, and the support of our family here at Leonard Petrew Junior High…" She was still at it. Ms. McCoy was leaning on her desk, trying to be patient while Mrs. Walker droned on.

Suddenly, I snapped to attention. What did she just say?

"…and to support one of our brightest stars, a boy who is courageously fighting a private battle with a life-threatening disease, our school will be holding a major fundraiser for the children's hospital. Or as I like to call it, a FUNdraiser!"

I was stunned! That was my private lie she was announcing to the whole school.

I sank down, my face burning, and scribbled madly with the Sharpie. Sometimes, even for a professional liar like me, it's hard to make your face look like you don't care. A whole FUNdraiser to support a liar like me?

Now, I knew the Monopoliitis lie was a big one. Obviously. I don't invent diseases every day of the week. I just didn't know it would turn into such a monster.

Wait: have I told you my theory about lying? Don't worry, this isn't a moral or a lesson or anything. It's just what I've noticed, in a detached, scientific way, in my own life of lies.

DR. SPIN'S THEORY OF LYING

Lies come in three main forms:

The One-Off (level: amateur)

This type of lie is small, quick and usually about something unimportant. Saying you brushed your teeth when you didn't is a typical lie of this level. Or that you ate your vegetables at lunch when you really two-pointed them into the garbage. A one-off lie might be as small as a yes or no. These lies often work well, especially when the person being lied to is busy, tired, uninterested or otherwise preoccupied.

The Multiplier (level: intermediate)

This type of lie builds on a smaller one, maybe a one-off, but requires further and more elaborate lies. It involves thinking quickly and improvising. For example:

Mom: "Did you do your homework?"

You: "Yep." First lie.

Mom: "Well, where is it?" .

You: "I finished it at school before the bell rang." Second lie, because it's sitting in your backpack.

Mom (*rummaging in your backpack, which is PRIVATE, but not really the point in this example*): "Well, what's this in your backpack, then?"

You: "Oh, that. Yeah, I still have to do *that*. But it's not for tomorrow. Our teacher said it's not due until Friday." Third lie, and possibly fourth.

The Monster (level: expert. Don't try this at home. Or at least really think it through before you try it.)

The monster is a lie not to be undertaken lightly. It is a huge lie, and it can have major, unexpected consequences. It can involve multipliers and can begin as a one-off, but it grows and grows out of the liar's control.

It is a dangerous kind of lying.

The Monopoliitis lie was obviously a monster. I'd known that when I decided to use it, but I'd foolishly thought I could control it. Me, the expert liar.

I'd been so busy warning Mrs. Walker not to talk to my mom about it that I'd forgotten to warn her not to talk to the *entire school*. She'd really caught me off guard on this one. Never for one moment did I think she would announce the news to the whole school or start a huge campaign about it. I thought she might discuss it generally at the next staff meeting or have a private word with my teachers. I never imagined how the whole situation could spiral out of control. How long would it be until everyone found out who the "sick" boy really was? Mrs. Walker-Talker was clearly not to be trusted.

That's the thing about lies. You have to be very, very good at them. You have to remember them. You have to track them. You have to plan. And even if you think you've done everything right (or, maybe, wrong?), they can still come back to bite you.

I know, I know: I deserve it.

But I didn't *expect* it.

→ INTERRUPTION BY MACY #4

"BoxyJoxy underwear seeks super-cute boy-spokes-model," read Macy.

I looked at her in horror.

"Don't...You...Dare," I whispered hoarsely.

She started laughing. Her laugh is sort of a snorting bellow.

"JOKE, Beauty Boy, I was JOKING! I made that one up! You shoulda seen your face! Ah, we do have fun, you and me, don't we?"

CHAPTER FOURTEEN

SHAY IS INTERESTED. TOO INTERESTED.

The FUNdraiser is taking over our school, which makes me swing wildly between worry and guilt. We seem to be spending a whole lot of class time on it. Not that I object to that part. That part would be fun, for a person not wracked with worry and guilt.

Chan and Frey and I make a point of calling it the FUN (you kind of shout that part out) draiser, just because *draiser* is such a cool word. We've decided that if we ever form a band (unlikely, because Frey and I play nothing and Chan only plays piano), we'll call it Draiser.

I'm avoiding Mrs. Walker and constantly pretending to be just another regular, healthy, concerned fellow student. Which, of course, I really *am*. It's so complicated.

Our class spent all morning painting banners for the event. You know, things like *Kids Care About Kids!* and *Fundraising for Life!* and *Being Sick Just Sucks!* (That last one was from the group I was in. All guys. Hey, we're in grade seven.)

Every penny of the money raised will go to the children's hospital, in case you're wondering. Can I feel less guilty because of that? Turns out, yes, I can! I actually feel good that we're doing something for sick kids, even though I don't happen to fit into that category.

In the middle of all this working together for a good cause, Shay is being more of a jerk than usual.

"I'm going to find out who it is," he told the class when Ms. McCoy got called to the office and we were "trusted to supervise ourselves." Why do teachers ever do that? We can't be trusted. I'll tell you that right now.

"The sick kid Walker was talking about. We should know. Maybe it's contagious or something. Anyway, I want to know who it is," he said, scanning the class. He looked at Edie, clearly wanting her to comment.

"Where's the black paint?" she asked, totally ignoring him and looking down at the banner they were making.

Shay started on Jamie, a thin, quiet guy in our class who takes *forever* to eat his sandwich at lunchtime.

I'm proud to say that while Shay was trying to bully Jamie into admitting his nonexistent illness, I "accidentally" splashed the pot of red paint I was carrying on Shay's shirt.

"Spin, you idiot!" he yelled.

"Oh, gee, Shay, sorry about that!" I dabbed at his shirt with the dirty rag I was carrying. "My bad."

He pulled furiously away from me and stalked out of the room. Edie caught my eye and smiled.

Shay had to change into his stinky gym shirt for the rest of the day! He'll get me back for that. But at the time, seeing his outraged little face was very sweet.

At lunch, Shay sat down at our table and started on Chan.

"So, Chan, how ya feeling?" he asked.

"Totally fine," said Chan, biting into an apple. "One hundred percent. Thanks for your concern though, Shay."

Shay looked over at Frey, big and solid, who was staring off into the distance, plowing his way through a mound of cookies. You could tell Shay rejected him immediately. He turned to me.

"Spin," he said, almost to himself, like he was considering me, "you're away a lot…" He studied me, his eyes narrowing.

"Never felt better, Shay. Hey, buddy, did you get that red paint out?" I asked, like I was all concerned about his shirt. The trick was to get Shay mad. He had a real temper and was easily distracted that way. You paid for it later, but whatever.

"No, moron," he snapped, getting up. "You owe me a shirt. A *good* one, not the loser crap you wear."

"Fair enough," I said. "What's your size?" I was feeling reckless.

"Medium!" he practically yelled. Now, it's certainly not something I brag about, but as a model, you get to know sizes. He was an extra small. Definitely.

"I don't have time for this," he said and walked away.

Mission accomplished.

Frey came out of his daydream, finished up his cookies and asked us if we were going to meet at Red Plush after school.

"I can't," I said, sighing. "I have a dentist appointment." Lie. I had to do some promo shoots Macy had lined up for my teen-model portfolio. Probably photos involving backward baseball caps. Adults still think those are cool.

"Me neither," said Chan. "Piano." Not a lie.

"Oh," said Frey, "because…"

We waited patiently. Frey takes his time.

"Because Red needs some help," he said. "Her son just moved to Vancouver, and he managed Red Plush, and the apartments Red owns across the park. So she's gotta do *that*, and take care of the video store…" This was quite a long speech for Frey. I think he was actually worried in his big, confused way.

"Anyway, I've got my paper route and hockey practice, but Mom and Dad told her that they'd ask around for her. See if anyone was interested in taking over from her son."

I thought about it. Red needed someone to help her. It seemed like it would be a great place to work: totally quiet, low-pressure, warm, good snacks. Sure, Red was kind of freaky-looking, but she was super nice.

I thought about my mom.

This just might make her business courses worth all the boredom. It would definitely be better than her job at the card store, which she always says is "just temporary."

Maybe Red Plush was Mom's big chance.

Maybe Red Plush was *our* big chance.

CHAPTER FIFTEEN

HEEEEERE'S CLARISSA, PSYCHO-FREAK GIRL MODEL

I can't believe my luck. Some people say that meaning "I'm so lucky!" You should know me and my life well enough by now.

Twice in four chapters I've had a shoot with Clarissa. It's like a one-two punch, or lightning striking twice, or having brussels sprouts two days in a row.

As usual, I'd thought this was a normal shoot, with normal people. Macy never tells me anything.

"Oh, you know, Nathan Stern, Nicole Nguyen, those kind of kids," she told me.

Yes, Nathan was there (he's a nice, serious kid who leans against the wall and reads during breaks), and yes, Nicole was there too, being talked at by Gilbert Sheppard. I like Nicole, and Gilbert's not a bad guy.

He just shares every little thought that rolls around in his brain. Anyway, all good, solid kid models. All nice, normalish people.

On the not-so-normal side, Clarissa was also there, sucking up to the photographer as usual.

It was a summer-catalog shoot with lots of bright lamps and bright clothes. I was gulping water by the tiny-paper-cupful and trying to ease the tight waist-band of my shorts.

We were all appreciating a short break from Clarissa.

In a mere one and a half hours, Clarissa had:

- Thrown a tantrum about her outfit until they scurried off to get her another one. I had this wicked waistband cutting into my body, and Nathan's shoes were clearly two sizes too big, but *she* got the new outfit.
- Pouted about the new outfit.
- Told me *very loudly* that Nathan should wash his hair more.
- Pushed Nicole out of the way. Hard.
- Told Gilbert to shut up (okay, we've *all* told Gilbert to shut up, but she said it in a very mean way).
- Cut Nicole out of one of the main shots by convincing Tony (the photographer) that it would be more effective with three (her in the middle, of course).

- Told me I stink (this may in fact be true, but, again, said with the meanness).
- Faked a twisted ankle. I know it was fake because I caught her limping on different sides. So I called out, "Hey, Clarissa, I thought you twisted your *right* ankle. But now you're limping on your *left* ankle. What's up with that?" All the other kids giggled. Clarissa glared at me.

I think we had everything but the fake-crying. Honestly, spending time with Clarissa makes you sort of fondly wish you were with normal, relaxing people like Shay.

Usually, kids who pull this kind of garbage don't go far in modeling. Photographers won't put up with it. I don't know why it works for Clarissa. Maybe the photographers are afraid of her. I know I am.

We started up again after the too-short break.

Tony had us all stand in a semicircle. We were supposed to stare upward, "amazed and delighted," and fake-laugh and fake-point at a sad little shriveled purple balloon they had hanging from a string.

"Focus on the balloon, kids! Amazement! Astonishment! That's it, that's it!" Tony called as he shot photo after photo.

Try it. Look up at your ceiling. Maybe there's a light there, or a bit of fluff, or an old spider web. Fixate on it. Now try to pretend it's something incredible, like maybe a spaceship or a flock of flamingos or...well, this is your thing—make something up. Now look amazed (your eyes should be open really wide; probably your mouth should be too) and point at the light/fluff/web. Feel kind of stupid? Yep, you're normal.

We all knew that in the catalog, we'd be pointing at something else. We just didn't know what. But for the time being, we looked up at the balloon and grinned and pointed.

Clarissa smiled brilliantly right into the camera.

"Suck in your guts, people," she said between clenched, perfect teeth. "I don't model with fat kids."

* * *

Macy took one look at my face when she picked me up, sighed and asked, "Clarissa act up again?"

"I'm never, ever modeling with her again, *ever*," I told Macy, flinging my bag into the backseat. I threw it hard. Like my stupid life was that bag's fault.

"I know, I know," Macy said soothingly. "She's temperamental. But you know, BB, Clarissa's got something.

Maybe it's those huge eyes...I don't know what it is, but she's magic on camera."

"I don't care!" I yelled. "I don't *care* about her eyes! I don't care about her magic! She's a freak! And I'm never, EVER modeling with her again."

Macy shrugged and left it there. Every once in a while, she has a bit of tact.

I thought I'd won.

Until I saw the entry on the calendar for the next Saturday: *S.H.F. shoot W/C.A. & C.J.* For those of you who haven't secretly researched and memorized Macy's abbreviations, I'll translate: *Shiny, Happy Family* shoot with Chad Adams and Clarissa Jamieson.

Now, I knew Macy had been working for years to get me into *Shiny, Happy Family*. It was a big magazine.

I knew it would be big money.

And I knew that somehow, some way, I wasn't going to be there.

CHAPTER SIXTEEN

HEY, SPORTS FANS: HOCKEY UPDATE!

So it's the first hockey practice after school today (he says casually, like the seasoned jock that he is). No big deal, right? Probably not for normal people, but I'm totally nervous and also wildly excited. It's all still hush-hush with Mom and Macy. They'd see all the problems with it, and I just don't need the hassle right now.

Good old Frey came to school with a stick and a huge hockey bag filled with equipment.

"Some gear for ya, Spin," he announced, dumping it on the floor next to my locker. "Me and Dad found a bunch of stuff that should sort of fit you. You even got matching gloves in there."

I was touched. I had always liked Mr. Frey, a big, shambling high-school shop teacher. But today, with a bag of hockey equipment at my feet, I loved the man.

I never knew a bag of hockey equipment weighed so much. I felt like a big hero just lifting it. (Okay, I secretly dragged it down the two long hallways leading into the arena, but I picked it up again before I staggered into the locker room.)

After being the fat boy in recent modeling shoots, it came as a nice surprise that all the equipment was pretty big. Very big. Frey-big. In fact, I used a spare pair of laces as a kind of belt for the pants. There was a massive, ancient set of hockey gloves, which looked like they were permanently clenched around an invisible hockey stick. There was a set of shoulder pads that made me look like a tank. Elbow pads, shin pads, knee pads—it didn't matter that they all ranged from extra large to monster-huge; the Freys had really helped me out.

There was even a gray shell-like thing with ropes on it. I studied it for a long time, then shrugged and chucked it back into the bag as the other guys burst into the room.

But not before Shay had seen me looking at it.

"In love with your gorgeous jockstrap, Spin?" he called.

Great. Shay's on the team.

Oh well, you can't have everything.

And at least I knew what the thing was. Of course, a couple of sticks to the groin and I would've figured it out.

I'm a quick learner.

* * *

"Okay, men, listen up," Coach bellowed. Coach called us men. I loved that. Coach was really Mr. Schulz, a short, roundish guy who taught grade-nine social studies. He wore an old ballcap and an ancient high-school football jacket.

"We have our first game earlier than expected, so we really have to get practicing. We're playing *this* Friday against the teachers, to wind up the school FUNdraiser."

He paused, looking around at our flushed, nervous faces.

"The whole school will be there; everyone's paying a buck to watch, so let's make it a good game."

My heart was pounding.

This FUNdraiser was ballooning into something pretty big. Mrs. Walker was more effective than I gave her credit for. She was like Macy: once you start them off, there's no stopping them.

We started out with drills. Skating, stickhandling, shooting. It was great being out there with Chan and Frey and all the other good guys. Even Shay couldn't ruin it for me.

"Good work, Spinelli," shouted Coach during one drill. One in which I *didn't* fall down. It's crazy how proud that made me. *Good work, Spinelli!* I repeated it in my head as I staggered and flailed my way down the ice. *GOOD work, Spinelli! Good WORK, Spinelli! Good work, SPINELLI!*

Do you do pathetic stuff like that in your head, or is it just me?

At the end of practice, Coach announced the lineup. I was made second-string defense, along with Chris Fedorek, who is also not much of a jock. Hey, I know it's not exactly the glamor position, but Chris and I had a lot of fun joking about our second-string defense line being a WALL OF PAIN.

"NONE SHALL PASS!" we bellowed, banging our sticks against the ice while the other guys on the team rolled their eyes.

Have I mentioned that I love hockey?

I peeled off the massive equipment, unlaced my skates and stuffed it all into my gym locker. My legs were quivering from all the exercise as I walked to the bus stop.

Reeking and steaming up the windows on the bus home, I thought about breaking it to Mom and Macy that I was on the school hockey team. I thought about all the hassles it was going to cause.

Then I remembered how fun practice had been. Hockey was worth fighting for. The simple right to play hockey. I think it might even be in the constitution somewhere.

I cleared a circle on the steamed-over window and looked out. The bus was just passing the Frey boys' rink, and several massive forms were gliding around out there in the dark.

I smiled.

Yep, it was all worth it.

→ INTERRUPTION BY MACY #5

"'Stylin' Cutz hair magazine seeks boy models with gorgeous hair.' Hey, this sounds like you, Beauty Boy!" Macy was, as usual, surfing the Internet for new and unique ways of torturing me.

"Blah, blah, blah, may require hair being cut, dyed, styled, blah, blah, blah, major national exposure with the possibility of an *extended contract*!" She was practically shouting. She swung around triumphantly.

I gave her a long look (a "steely glare" in modeling speak) and walked out of the room.

"What a grouch!" I heard Macy say to Mom. "You figure it's hormones? It's GOT to be hormones."

CHAPTER SEVENTEEN

MOM AND MACY FREAK OUT ABOUT THE HOCKEY RIGHT ON CUE (DIDN'T I PREDICT THIS?)

I had to tell Mom and Macy about being on the hockey team. It's not like I suddenly came to a mature decision about not lying anymore. If I could have, I would've let it go as long as possible. Unfortunately, I had early-morning practice the next day, and I could hardly bolt out of the house at 6:00 AM without some kind of explanation.

We were eating dinner. Well, Macy and Mom were eating. I was pushing a watery piece of fish around islands of broccoli on my plate. Macy was ranting about some company she was fighting with. It was amazing how much food she seemed to be able to shovel in while she talked. It wasn't pretty. Eventually, she took a breath or swallowed, and I jumped in.

"Hey, I've been wondering about something," I began. "Did Dad play sports?"

It wasn't just a random question. This was a carefully planned attack.

"BB, you never saw such an athlete as your dad," said Macy, putting down her fork.

Mom saw Macy gearing up for another long reminiscence about Big BB and quickly said, "He played basketball in high school. Volleyball too. All the tall sports."

"How about hockey? Did he ever play hockey?"

"Yep. Defense," she said. This surprised me.

"He wasn't *great* at hockey though," she laughed, remembering. "He wasn't much of a skater. Couldn't really stop properly. But he was big."

"He skated *beautifully*," argued Macy, who had very likely never seen him skate, "like a...like a..." She flailed a bit, trying to think of something that skates incredibly well. "Like a PRO!" she finished triumphantly.

Mom shrugged, smiling.

I swallowed.

"That's interesting," I said loudly, "because I play hockey now too. On the school team. Defense. Just like Dad." Strange how saying that actually made me proud.

Mom and Macy erupted together.

"You WHAT?"

"Why didn't you *tell* us?"

"Do you have a proper helmet?"

"Your *face*, Beauty Boy, your beautiful *FACE!*" This was Macy, of course.

Are you beginning to see why I kept it from them? I thought of breakaways and slap shots. They thought of injuries and head shots. My whole life long, the threat of an accident had put so many activities out of bounds. Like going on a trampoline, tobogganing, rock climbing, even bike riding.

Mom saw the look on my face.

"Sorry, Luke. We should have said congratulations on making the team! That's quite an accomplishment."

I didn't think I needed to tell her that any breathing body made the team.

"Thanks, Mom. It's only for one tournament," I explained, "and one game against the teachers."

"This is TOTALLY STUPID!" Macy burst out. "One puck in the face and POOF! There goes your whole modeling career! Ever thought of that, BB?"

Oh, yes, Macy, I thought, *as a matter of fact I have thought of that. I can only hope.*

"Look, it's done," I said. "Frey's loaned me some equipment, and Chan and his dad are picking me up for early-morning practice tomorrow." I pushed back my chair and got up. "And you know what?

Even though I'm not much good, I love it! I love being on the team!"

I ran to my room and slammed the door. Not very mature, I know, but sometimes a door-slam is very satisfying.

* * *

Macy cornered me in the hall just before bedtime. She gave me one of her smother-hugs, crushing me against her shoulder.

"BB, I'm sorry," she said unexpectedly. "Congrats on making the team, you superstar athlete you!" She sort of cuffed my head gently, then grabbed my face in her big hand.

"Just take care of this gorgeous face." She gave my face a little squeeze and a shake. "We have big plans for this face!"

"Okay, okay," I protested, squirming away from her.

I watched her lumber back down the hall.

Yes, Macy, I thought, *I have big plans for this face too. And they don't involve modeling. They involve pizza.*

CHAPTER EIGHTEEN

MIDDLE-OF-THE-COLD-DARK-NIGHT HOCKEY PRACTICE

I'm not a morning person.

Early morning (any time on the clock that starts with a five or a six) is particularly horrible. It's practically the middle of the night.

Anyway, early-morning hockey practice sounded like much more fun than it was. Chan and his dad picked me up at 6:15 AM. It was still dark outside, and very cold. The kind of cold where you see every breath you exhale; the kind of cold that reminds you how often we really breathe. It seemed very heroic, leaving a warm house to crunch out to hockey practice in the middle of the night like this.

Chan's dad jumped out of the van. He's got trendy glasses, a big smile and tons of energy. He made it feel like we were going off on an exciting trip.

"'Morning, Luke! Hi, Kathy!" he called, reaching for my enormous bag of enormous equipment and stowing it away for me.

"'Morning, Edwin!" called my mom from the door. "Brrr. What a morning! Hey, thanks for giving Luke a ride."

"Oh, no problem." He looked surprised, like who wouldn't want to be up at the crack of dawn, driving kids to hockey practice?

"Yeah, thanks, Dr. Chan," I said, "Bye, Mom."

"Have fun!" She gave a hurried wave and shut the door.

The Chan van was wonderfully warm as I slid into the backseat. I had bed head and huge bags under my red-rimmed eyes, and I was barely thinking at all. Chan was completely awake, alert and ready to talk.

"See the game last night, Spin? I had hockey practice, but we got home sort of mid-second period." He rattled on about the game as the mindless morning radio blared. As we turned left onto the main street, I marveled, in a slow and sluggish way, at how many people were up in the middle of the night.

Chan's dad started talking cheerfully about some junior hockey player he'd seen recently for some disgusting rash. I only caught parts of it.

"...raised and pus-filled..."

"...had to cut his shirt sleeve right off..."

"...creeping up his neck onto the side of his *face*..."

Both of Chan's parents are very enthusiastic dermatologists. You have to be prepared for rash-talk (and worse) when you're with skin doctors. I looked at the back of Dr. Chan's head as he chattered about boils, pus, rashes, sores and blood. My 6:00 AM Cheerios lurched dangerously around inside me. I looked out the window, and tried to tune out Mr. Chan's rash-chatter.

Finally, several scabby patients later, we pulled up at the arena across the street from our school. A black BMW slid in behind us. Shay and his dad. Shay has mentioned his dad's Beamer about four thousand times at school.

Mr. Chan was just finishing up his last story about a monstrous pustule that had required some totally putrid digging and draining.

"...six stitches to close it!"

"Wow! Six!" Chan squirmed excitedly at this disgusting fact.

I looked out the back window at the Beamer. I'd never seen Shay's dad before, and I was curious. He was just an average-looking guy in a suit, with slicked-back hair, talking on his cell phone. *Who is he talking to in the middle of the night?* I wondered. Shay got out of the car, walked around to the trunk and waited. And waited. Finally, he knocked on the trunk, just once, just one of those one-knock, open-up kind of things you do to let a driver know you need the trunk opened.

The knock did not go over well.

Shay's dad swiveled around and glared at Shay before he popped the trunk. Shay dug his bag out, and the Beamer fishtailed off, his dad still glued to his cell phone.

Now, I'm not expecting to see hugs and kisses every time a parent drops his kid off. Nobody wants that. But maybe eye contact? Maybe not letting your kid wait in the bitter cold until he has to *knock*? I knew my dad wouldn't have dropped me off like that.

Dr. Chan did one of those exaggerated *oof* sounds as he heaved my gigantic equipment bag. "What do you have in here, a *body*?" he said. We all laughed.

Shay looked over as he walked by.

"Hey, Shay," I said.

"Hi," he said shortly, without stopping.

I watched him walk toward the big white arena doors, just a little dark shadow in the gloom, getting smaller and smaller.

CHAPTER NINETEEN

TRUTH. HMMM, I'M NOT SO GOOD AT THIS.

It was the night before the FUNdraiser. I imagined another day of avoiding Mrs. Walker's increasingly obvious smiles and glances. Another day of trying to stop Shay from finding out that I was the fake-sick kid who started the whole thing. And if I lived through tomorrow, the next day was the *Shiny, Happy Family* shoot with Chad and Clarissa. My life was getting better and better.

I lay in my bed trying to convince my body to become really, really sick. Getting really sick would solve all of my immediate problems. I wouldn't get to play in the hockey game, but, to be honest, playing the first official game of my life in front of the entire school terrified me.

Getting hot...
Think feeevvvver...
Think sore throat...

I was interrupted by a soft knock on the door. Mom. When Macy knocked, she hammered so hard it sounded like a construction crew.

"Come in," I said.

"Hey," she said, coming into the room. "Whoa, it's cold in here! Can I close that window? You'll catch pneumonia!"

That was the plan.

Mom sat down on the side of the bed and smoothed my hair from my annoyingly non-feverish forehead.

"Are you feeling okay?" she asked, looking concerned.

"Yeah," I said. She looked tired.

"How about you?" I asked. "How's work?"

"Oh, all right," she said. "New manager's driving me crazy though."

Then I remembered about Red Plush. Mom and I hadn't had much time to talk since I'd broken the hockey news, but I felt guilty that I'd forgotten to tell her what Frey said.

"Hey, Mom," I said, propping myself up on one elbow, "I know a place where you might get a job. One you'd like. It's a really cool place." I ended up telling her all about Red and the store, and how it was near the school and Frey's family and the rink.

She listened. My mom was a good listener. She didn't fidget or look away or bite her nails or anything. She just sat there, looking at me encouragingly.

"This woman's name is Red?" she asked. "Just Red?"

"I guess she must have a last name," I said, wondering what on earth it could be. Not Plush. Surely not Plush. Anyway, I had never heard it.

"Well, thanks," she said, smiling. "I've got a day off tomorrow. I might pop over to this Red Plush. Sounds fun."

She looked at me and then blurted out, "You want to quit modeling, don't you?"

I stared at her.

"I *know* you want to quit. I don't want you to think you're letting me or Macy down. I want you to tell me the truth."

The truth.

"I'm not so good at the truth, Mom," I said.

She laughed.

"Try it," she said.

I took a deep breath. It was hard to get started. But once I did, I got going pretty quickly. I told her the truth. I told her everything.

I told her that if I had to do one more stupid pose, I would scream the place down. I told her that I'd had it with fake-smiling, fake-laughing, fake-running and fake everything. I told her about Chad's hair and Clarissa's psycho-freakiness and lying to my friends and how frustrating it was to not have a real life.

I told her how scared I was that Shay would find out about the modeling. I told her about letting her down by lying when she had trusted me. I told her about talking to the principal and how the monster lie was taking on a life of its own. And I told her I felt sick about the FUNdraiser the next day and the *Shiny, Happy Family* shoot the day after that.

I looked away from Mom's face as I talked. She wanted the truth. She asked for it.

I talked a lot. Even for me. I talked until there was no more talk left in me. Finally, I lay back against my pillows and closed my eyes. Who knew telling the truth was so exhausting?

"Well," I said, "there you go. You'll never ask me to tell the truth again, hey?"

She sat very still.

"Actually," she said, "we're going to have nothing but the truth starting now. Thanks for being honest, BB. Sorry. *Luke*. I'm so sorry you've been so miserable. You should have told me. I've noticed lately that you've been sort of moody and unhappy, but Macy and I thought it must just be teenage stuff. You know. I was a teenage terror, so I guess I thought all teenagers go through that."

"Well, give me time," I said. "I'm not actually, officially, a teenager yet. Watch out though. Birthday coming up." We laughed a little. Then Mom smoothed my hair.

"Things will be different now, I promise. Okay?"

"Okay," I said. But I wasn't convinced. Macy the Tank stood in the way of our freedom.

Mom gave me a hug. I felt a little better.

I heard her and Macy talking in the family room. Soft voice, then big RUMBLE, then soft voice, then RUMBLE. They were still talking when I fell asleep.

Nothing would change. Neither one of us was as strong or as determined as Macy.

But at least now it was two against one.

CHAPTER TWENTY

THE FUNDRAISER DAY OPENS WITH A BANG (BRACE YOURSELF. IT'S UGLY.)

Mom and Macy were up and out of the house when my alarm went off. This was highly unusual.

Mom had left a note for me.

Luke,

I have a bunch of stuff I have to do today, so thought I'd get an early start. Macy's at a breakfast meeting with some client. Don't worry about anything. We had a long talk, and it's all under control. Talk to you later.

Love, Mom

PS: Eat some breakfast. Here's money for lunch.

Yeah, right. All under control. When had either of us ever been able to control Macy?

It was one of those days when the weather doesn't seem to understand that you're very depressed and that your life is a tangled, stupid mess. It was a clear-blue, sparkling day with frost decorating every tree branch.

I stared dully out the bus window at the winter wonderland and wondered how I was going to get through the day without being revealed as the phony sick kid, and how I was going to get through the *next* day fake-smiling with Chad and Clarissa.

So I was totally unprepared for the bomb when it fell. To those of you literal kids who just jumped to your feet thinking, No way! A BOMB went off?!: relax. And sit down. This is not that kind of book.

All I meant was that something really, really bad happened. And I wasn't ready for it. We clear on that? No actual bombs.

As I turned down the hall to my classroom, Chan hurried up to me with a bunch of papers in his hand.

"Not good, Spin, not good. In fact," he added, shoving the papers at me, "probably really, really bad. I took down as many of them as I could, but look…" He gestured down the hall, where sheets of paper were taped to every locker, every door, every window.

I looked down at the paper. It was a photocopy of one of my modeling shoots from about six years ago. It was for a bridal magazine, and I was a fake ring bearer.

I was wearing fake glasses and a small (and, as I recall, too-tight) tuxedo with a fake flower in the buttonhole. I was holding a small pillow with a fake wedding ring stuck on it, smiling up at the women around me. The fake bride and all her fake brides-maids were smiling down at me. It hadn't been a bad shoot. Everyone had been nice.

But let's face it: it's not the kind of thing you really expect to see papering the walls of your junior high when you are busy worrying about your fake sickness.

Someone had written GUESS WHO?? at the top of the page.

I looked around. The photocopies were everywhere.

It had come.

Doom.

The moment I'd been dreading my whole life.

Through the rising panic, I heard my brain say, *You still have time to run! The bell hasn't rung yet!*

But somehow, my feet started walking toward the classroom.

What are you guys doing? screamed my brain at my feet. *Crisis here! Run! RUN AWAY!*

My feet don't hear very well, apparently. They walked all the way down the hall to the classroom. Past kids who were whispering and grinning and staring. Past nice girls looking sorry for me, past guys looking guiltily relieved that they weren't going to be today's victims.

Frey swung around from his locker, saw me and said through the apple in his mouth, "Hey, Spin! Hockey today!" Apparently he hadn't noticed the three thousand sheets of paper covering all the nearby surfaces.

I managed a smile. Good old Frey.

Hockey today. He was right. Today was my first hockey game ever. Coach was even buying us pizza after the game. In the midst of my life shattering and crumbling into dust, I'd forgotten that fact. It made me feel better. Frey caught up with Chan and me, and we all walked into the classroom together. Did they wait to walk in with me to help me out? Did they walk in with me because they knew it'd be hard? I'll never really know. But at that moment, walking in with my friends was WAY better than walking in alone.

Shay was waiting. The whole class was waiting. There was a stillness in the air.

"Well, GUESS WHO's here?" shouted Shay, his evil little face bright and expectant.

"Hey, Shay," I said casually, dumping my backpack on my chair.

He frowned.

Ahhh, I thought. *The trick is to stay casual.* Hard when your heart is pounding and your face feels hot.

I pretended I needed all my concentration for unpacking my backpack. But ignoring Shay never made Shay go away.

"Have you happened to notice this *gorgeous* photo, Spin?" Shay could barely contain his glee. He slammed one of the posters on my desk, right underneath my face.

"Check out the little guy in the tux! He's SOOOOO cute!"

I turned and looked at him. What I saw wasn't pretty. He was going to humiliate me as much as he could. He was going to torture me.

And then something in me snapped.

I'd had all I could take.

Here I was, caught in this monster lie, doomed to model endlessly, and Shay was determined to humiliate me, to beat me to a pulp, mind-bully style.

Well, it wasn't going to happen.

There's a depressing song my mom used to play, and one of the lines is *When you ain't got nothing, you got nothing to lose.* Or something like that. That's how I felt. I had nothing to lose. Rock bottom. Maybe it sounds pathetic, but when you hit rock bottom, you realize there's nowhere to go but up. All my nervousness and fear melted away. I felt oddly calm.

I smiled, as if he was paying me a genuine compliment. It was one of those hard, stiff smiles that had no humor in it. It was a smile that said, *Watch out, Shay, I'm coming for you.*

"Aw, thanks, Shay," I said loudly. "You know, you just might fit into that little tux in a few years. Like, for grad or something. I can see if they still have it."

There was dead silence. Everyone looked stunned. Nobody talked like that to Shay. Even Frey stopped chewing and just stood there with a mouthful of apple.

I continued. Recklessly.

"And you never told us you had a subscription to *Bridal Dreaming* magazine!" I said. "That's where the photo came from. Dreaming about being a bride, Shay?"

Some of the kids started to snigger, and all of a sudden the room felt less tense.

"At least I'm not *starring* in it," Shay said. He had a point, and he knew it.

He leaned in closer, in mock concern.

"Tell us, Spin, how it feels to be a boy model. We would really *love* to see some of your other, more recent, work."

You know me pretty well by now. I may be a lot of things, but I'm not stupid. There was no way I was going to blab my life story because Shay had got hold of one photograph. *He has one photo. ONE*, I kept reminding myself.

But there're about two million more he could dig up soon, a tiny voice in my brain said. *When that website of Macy's goes live.* I hate that tiny brain voice. It never, ever whispers good things.

I hesitated.

Edie came in. She picked up the sheet on her desk, looked at it and sighed.

"Oh, wait, don't tell me," she said in her slow, bored voice. She closed her eyes and put her fingers to her forehead like she was telling our fortunes.

"Spin does this thing when he was a little kid, probably because his mom forced him to, and Shay's torturing him about it. Am I right?" Have I mentioned that Edie is *the* coolest girl in school?

She looked around. Some kids nodded, grinned and started to drift away to their own desks.

"Yep, Edie. Bingo," said Chan.

Edie glanced over at Shay. "You're so boringly predictable," she said, stifling a yawn.

Shay sensed that he was losing the edge in the confrontation. This made him aggressive.

"I'm just asking Little Mr. Ring Bearer here how long he's been secretly modeling, that's all." Shay was always better behaved with Edie around. He made it sound as if it were a serious, legitimate question.

The whole class looked over at me expectantly.

It was now or never.

"Oh, probably for as long as you've been reading *Bridal Dreaming*, Shay," I said.

There was a beat of silence, then everyone laughed. Even Edie.

The bell rang. I couldn't believe I had got the last line in. Okay, I couldn't believe I even *thought* of a last line, let alone a pretty good one.

Ms. McCoy came in, looking mad.

"Who is responsible for the state of the hall and this classroom?" She picked up one of the sheets. "'Guess Who?' What is this? Well, obviously, it's Luke." She looked over at me. "Cute picture, Luke. Somebody else must have thought so too, having run off what looks like several hundred copies. It better not have been on the school photocopier."

She turned to Shay wearily.

"Shay, this is obviously your work. I know your handwriting. Go and collect every single last one of these and put them in the recycle bin in the teachers' lounge. And don't touch anything else in there. Or eat anything. Actually, just give them to Mrs. Barnes at the office desk. Then report to the principal. As usual."

"No problem, Ms. M., got it covered," Shay said, like he was being very helpful. "I'll be a *model* student," he added from the doorway, giving the class a big wink. You have to hand it to Shay. He's quick.

Everyone laughed. Shay probably wanted it to be mean laughter. But it wasn't.

It was just normal laughter.

CHAPTER TWENTY-ONE

I INVENT A NEW VERSION OF DODGEBALL (ALL HEAD SHOTS ALL THE TIME)

Never, *ever* has a day been so long.

Well, maybe it has been for guys at war, or people trapped in an avalanche, or kids forced to visit really, really boring relatives…But you know what I mean. It was the longest day for *me*. It was unbelievably long.

Shay called me Tux whenever he saw me and kept mock-framing me with his hands like he was taking pictures.

I infuriated him by asking him bridal trivia. "Hey, Shay, what's new in veils?" or "Quick, Shay: three tips for a winter wedding!" It was all very childish. Tiring too. Because every time I asked him some bridal question, I had to think up another one for the next time he bugged me.

My recklessness was melting away. Worry moved in, stretched and settled down on my mental couch. Shay had obviously just come across that photo by accident. I didn't know where: doctor's office? Dentist's? Who stocked magazines that old? But you could bet that he'd be googling my name to dig up more dirt. And when Macy finalized her website, it would be disastrous; he would see every photo I'd ever had taken. Every shoot. *Everything*.

Models by Macy would bury me.

* * *

My class had the whole afternoon to visit the FUNdraiser events.

There was a "penny carnival" in the cafeteria, where for mere pennies (okay, every game was at least twenty-five cents) you could win fantastic prizes like dollar-store pencils or hair elastics or a tiny bouncy ball. I won two pens, a small bottle of shampoo and a travel-size deodorant.

The grand prize was a huge basket of shampoos and soaps (notice the slightly insulting personal-hygiene theme), which Frey won. He quickly traded it to Angela Boyko, who'd won a gift certificate for a large pepperoni pizza. Both of them looked totally satisfied with the trade.

Even with all the excitement of winning small personal-grooming products, it was hard to stay happy. Whenever I stopped moving, I started worrying.

I was with a group of guys who were laughing and talking and enjoying our day without classes. I got quieter and quieter. I felt alone and depressed.

But, hey, nothing like a little enforced dodgeball to cheer a fella up! There was a mandatory, school-wide tournament, homeroom versus homeroom. Each homeroom collected two dollars per student for the FUNdraiser.

Dodgeball.

The ultimate contest of strength and agility. The purest form of sport. The...

Okay, it's just a goofy game where kids smack each other with balls and race around like crazy. Most kids love it. Usually I did, too, but right at this moment it seemed kind of pointless.

We started against 7D. 7D was Tyson Kemp's homeroom. You remember Tyson Kemp? Way back in chapter 6 he made a brief appearance as exhibit A in my demonstration of how bullies have changed over the years. He's the freakishly big former bully who is still as strong as a gorilla.

Tyson Kemp lived for dodgeball. It was the only semilegal violence the school still allowed.

He took out all his math-related frustrations on the opposing team. He fired the ball so hard it stung. And, predictably, he played dirty. He made dodge-ball a blood sport.

It was pure chaos in the gym, kids yelling and running and balls flying and people getting pelted. Tyson was picking us off like a sniper. I saw Chan crumple after a particularly nasty head shot, his glasses skidding across the gym floor. As I picked them up, I thought that pretty much the only rule in dodgeball is "no head shots," right? Really, if you were to look in the dodgeball rulebook, there'd only be one rule: no head shots.

Well, Tyson was all head shots all the time. He made a *point* of throwing at people's heads. Even when he had a clear body shot—a wide-open back, for example—he'd go for the head.

So anyway, I was hovering at the back of our side, watching all of Tyson's cheap head shots, when it hit me (no lame pun intended). Here, right here in this gym, was my chance to get out of tomorrow's modeling shoot!

A head shot could easily be a *face* shot, couldn't it? Wouldn't it be a shame if my face got in the way of one of Tyson's throws? Wouldn't it break some-thing, or swell up something awful? So bad that, say, any modeling this weekend, and possibly for weeks afterward, would have to be cancelled? That would be such a pity.

Okay, it wasn't a *perfect* idea. Maybe it was even a seriously flawed one. But it was *an* idea. I didn't have any others, and I was getting desperate. I somehow didn't feel quite so depressed now that I had this little project to work on.

I dropped my ball and concentrated on throwing myself face-first in front of every ball Tyson threw. I must have looked like a total freak out there, throwing myself all over the place, mostly headfirst.

"Thanks, Spin," panted Chelsea as I took a ball to the chest that was aimed at her head.

"You rock, Spin," yelled Mario as my right shoulder saved him from a killer Tyson shot.

Every time I came back in, I took hits all over my body, but it was like there was some sort of invisible shield over my face.

The whistle finally blew to end the game. My shoulders sagged. Just my luck. My face hadn't even *touched* a ball. Not even close.

All of a sudden, a ball rocketed at my head, thumping me hard enough that I fell to my knees. This is something you don't expect to happen when the *whistle has blown*.

I picked my dazed self up and looked around. Tyson was grinning right at me.

You moron, I thought. *Can't you do anything right?* I didn't know if my brain voice was talking to Tyson or to myself.

I'd finally got my head shot. I'd certainly have a huge bruise and a large bump.

Completely invisible, under my hair, on the *back* of my head.

CHAPTER TWENTY-TWO

I HAVE A VERY CLOSE SHAVE (AND BY THAT I MEAN B-A-L-D)

After lunch, we went to the gym. The teachers had opened the outside doors to air out the smell of dodgeball and set up another bunch of FUNdraiser activities. Ms. McCoy pointed them out.

"Okay, class, on your left: bake sale, popcorn station and dunk tank! Whoops, there goes Mr. Kowalski!" she laughed as the sound of a teacher hitting water filled the gym.

Mr. Kowalski was just climbing out of the tank, the strands of the hair he usually combed over the top of his head straggling like wet seaweed down the side of his face. The guy from grade eight who'd dunked him was grinning and being high-fived by the other kids in the line.

"And on your right," Ms. McCoy continued, "face painting, fake tattoos and, for any brave folks who've filled out a sponsor sheet, the head-shaving station."

Wait a second. What was that? What was that last one?

Headshaving station...

I stared. A kid in grade nine was sitting there in one of those hair-salon smocks, grinning, while a hairdresser shaved off half of his long hair. A bunch of kids were cheering and clapping. I ran over and grabbed a pamphlet.

Blah, blah, blah, money goes to the children's hospital, blah, blah, blah, sponsors, blah, blah, blah, *head shaved*. It was perfect! Here was something worthwhile (who can argue against helping sick kids?) that would result in me being completely bald. BALD! I was pretty sure being bald would get me out of that shoot tomorrow. Not much of a market for bald kids in advertising.

I must have been away when they handed out the sponsorship forms, so I grabbed one and took it into the corner of the room. I had brought sixty-two dollars of my own money to contribute to the FUNdraiser (not only because I felt horribly guilty about starting this whole thing off but because it was a great cause). This seemed like the perfect way to donate it.

It had to look believable. I used three different pens and changed my writing so it looked like I'd walked around and got different people to sponsor me. I put down Mom for twenty dollars, Macy for ten and our neighbor, Mrs. Fitzpatrick, for ten. Then I added five dollars from Red and five from Dan, who cuts the grass at our building. So that's...fifty bucks, right? I put down myself for the last twelve.

Then I took the form to the woman at the table.

My heart was pounding.

"Okay, hon," she said. "Good timing. Sheila's free."

As I walked over to the chair, some girls from my class who were at the fake-tattoo booth called, "Spin! You're doing the headshave?"

"Yep," I said casually, "can't wait. I'm all sponsored-up and everything."

"Ah, another victim," grinned Sheila, sweeping up the hair from under her chair.

She sat me down and put a plastic cape around my neck.

"Gorgeous hair, buddy. Nice and thick and curly," she said. "Well, here's your last chance. You sure about this?"

I looked at her in the mirror they'd propped up in front of the bleachers.

"Oh, yeah," I said. "Totally, totally sure."

Most of my class had heard I was doing the head-shave and gathered around the chair. It was quite a party atmosphere. Shay was there too. He was unusually quiet. I called over to him.

"Hey, Shay, take a picture!"

He turned and stalked away, probably to dunk some teacher.

My class started up a "bald" chant. The tune was sort of like the organ at hockey games, only here, they repeated the word "BALD" slowly at first, then quicker and quicker, ending in a loud "BALD!!"

Sheila held the clippers up high and got the class to count down from five.

"Five! Four! Three! Two! One! SHAVE!"

Now, I'm no stranger to the clippers, but this was *nothing* like the weekly haircuts I get from Scott, Macy's "hair wizard." Scott always looks really busy, but I sometimes think he's just back there making snippy-clippy sounds behind my head. How much hair can you actually trim every *week*?

This was the exact opposite of a trim.

The clippers came down and shaved a line right down the center of my head. Whoa! That first line of baldness felt weird and scary and exciting at the same time. The class cheered as row after row of my dark hair slid onto the floor.

Becoming bald was quite an interesting sensation.

It didn't take very long—less time than it takes to get a haircut, that's for sure. I guess that when you're shaving a head, you don't have to be all picky about lengths and getting things even. You just fire that sucker back and forth, and presto, you've got a bald head in front of you.

And there I was. In the mirror. Totally bald. I tilted my head from side to side. Yep, pure baldness. Without my hair, my nose looked bigger, my eyebrows darker, my head huger and whiter. I was delighted.

I shook Sheila's hand, high-fived all the kids in the class and then borrowed Chan's cell phone.

I ran into the hall where it was quiet. The air felt cold whirling around my bald head.

"Good afternoon. Models by Macy, Macy Spinelli speaking," said Macy in her fake smooth, professional phone voice.

"Hi, Macy, it's me. Got some news," I said, sounding very important.

"Oh, hi, Beauty," she said, dropping back into her regular voice. "What's up, kiddo?" She sounded distracted. I could hear computer keys clicking in the background.

"I shaved my head."

"WHAT!"

"My head. My hair. It's all shaved off." I was enjoying this moment so much. So very, very much. I couldn't stop smiling. "We had a fundraiser for sick kids, and I shaved my entire head."

There was silence at the other end of the phone. *Oh, Macy, do I have your attention now?*

"You're joking," she said finally.

"Nope!" I said cheerfully. "I'm completely bald here! Not a hair on my head."

There was another silence. I held the phone about a foot from my ear, waiting for the explosion.

"Oh, Beauty, you're such a good little guy," Macy said quietly. She sounded as if she was going to cry. "Did you really do that for charity? Such a generous guy…"

I couldn't believe it.

"So, you're not mad?" I said tentatively.

"Mad? Somebody does something so beautiful, and I'm supposed to be mad?" she asked, sniffling.

I have to admit, I didn't expect this reaction. Yelling, yes. Arguing, definitely. Crying, not at all.

"I won't be able to do the shoot tomorrow, I guess," I sighed, pretending to be sort of sorry about it.

"Oh, that," Macy said, as if it was unimportant. "Don't you worry about *that*, Beauty. Besides," she said with a laugh, "I know a good wig place. See ya, sweetie."

And she hung up.

Leaving me standing there, staring at the phone, bald and confused.

CHAPTER TWENTY-THREE

BREAKING NEWS: TEACHER-STUDENT HOCKEY GAME ENDS IN BLOODBATH

It was the third period in the FUNdraiser hockey game against the teachers.

We were in the arena across the street from the school, and pretty much the whole school was there. They kind of had to be. The teachers were either playing or cheering. That's not to say that everyone was paying attention. We're in junior high, remember. Kids were mostly running up and down the stands, throwing popcorn at each other. You know, regular stuff.

To be honest with you, it hadn't been a very good game so far. Mr. Bruseker, the phys ed teacher, was killing us single-handedly.

Hey, Mr. B., if you're trying to impress anyone (like, for example, Mademoiselle Lamont, the new French teacher), she might have happened to notice that *you're playing against children*. Just a tip.

I'd mostly sat on the bench with Chris "Wall of Pain" Fedorek, just watching the game and banging my stick against the boards whenever our team did something right. There was a lot of pressure playing in front of the whole school. Most of the guys were pretty nervous, though Coach was trying to keep it light and fun.

Shay had spent most of the game screaming at the defensemen. Forwards like Shay always assumed that if they just *got the puck*, it was practically guaranteed to be in the net within seconds. We all knew that he'd had lots of chances, but Mr. B. (the man who plays every position) had shut him down.

It was 4–0 for the teachers, even though the principal, Mrs. Walker, had finally benched Mr. B. early in the second period. She'd taken his place.

I hadn't talked to Mrs. Walker since my monster lie. I had successfully avoided her in the halls. The trick was to walk fast with your head down, or hide in a group of people when you walked past her office.

Mrs. Walker was sort of at my level, as a player. She could mostly stay upright, but she flailed a lot too.

And there were problems stopping. Always with the stopping, hey?

Anyway, Shay had come out of position to scream at the defense when the puck got flipped to where he was supposed to be. Chan tore after it, flicking it farther before crashing into the boards. Frey, for some reason, was circling slowly around in their end. He was *really* slow getting back on defense, so he might still have been there from a few plays ago. He sort of swung around at exactly the right moment and cracked the puck straight through Mr. Sharma's legs and into the net.

We went wild! GOAL! And by Frey, a defenseman! It was almost too good to be true. Frey skated calmly back to his position like nothing had happened, but I could tell he was happy. Chan was body-slamming him, falling down, picking himself up and body-slamming him again. Chris and I leaned over the boards, banging them with our sticks like real hockey players.

Shay looked like murder at center ice. A real team player, I thought. A real buddy.

And can you believe it? We popped in two more goals that period! And Shay didn't score either of them! It was 4–3 as the final minutes ticked away.

I was actually on the ice for the last few minutes. Frey needed a rest, and Chris's asthma was acting up from all the excitement, so Coach called on Spin. The Spinster. The Spinmeister. Old Spineroo. I clambered out of the box, my heart pounding.

"What?" screamed Shay, flying past. "We're bringing on the losers now?? I'd take a dead body out here over that guy!"

I ignored him. You had to. I'm happy to say that I navigated over to my position without falling down. For me, that was quite an achievement.

I turned to see Danny McRea shoot from the blue line, a weird, rolling shot that hopped over Mr. Sharma's glove. It was a tie! 4–4! I prayed the puck would stay in their end for a while. There was only a minute and a half left. Our guys were scrambling to keep it near the teachers' net, and on the teachers' bench, Mr. Bruseker was practically bursting a blood vessel.

"Change lines! CHANGE LINES!" he screamed. "SUB! *SUB!*"

Out of the scrum, with seconds left on the clock, Ms. Borelli flipped the puck to center line, and Mrs. Walker tore after it. She managed to push it farther down toward the defense line. Jacob, the other defender, lunged toward it and missed, sprawling on the ice and sailing right into the boards.

The next bit is kind of a blur.

I was the only thing left between our net and the puck. How scary is that? I never realized defense was such a tense position. I always thought you were kind of safe, tucked away at the back, away from the drama at center ice.

Mrs. Walker skated toward the puck, panting, her eyes wild behind her thick glasses and her grill. Everyone was screaming—Shay, Mr. B., the guys on the bench, even some kids in the crowd who weren't throwing popcorn at each other.

I gritted my teeth and skated toward Mrs. Walker with my stick out. As I got closer, I saw that her freak-ishly fast skating was totally out of control. I saw panic in her eyes as she tried to slow down.

She came right at me like a tank on ice.

Like I said, this part is kind of a blur, but people have told me what happened. We crashed into each other in a flailing ball of arms and legs and sticks. And as we fell, Mrs. Walker's skates slipped completely out from under her, and her arms came straight out in a desperate attempt to balance herself.

And her stick crashed against my helmet. Upward. Hard.

There were two cracking sounds.

The first was my old helmet's rusted grill tearing off.

The second was my nose breaking.

* * *

I lay there bleeding all over the ice. You know the worst nosebleed you've ever had? Multiply that by about nine thousand. It's hard to imagine that a nose can bleed that much blood and still stay a nose, but, yep, as it turns out, it can. I've been told by kids who were up in the stands that all that blood looked very dramatic against the white ice. Not only did Mrs. Walker's stick break my nose, it split my lip. Lots of blood.

I heard people yelling. Someone—I think it might have been Mrs. Walker—was sobbing and saying, "Oh, NO! Oh, NO!"

I could see a circle of heads looking down at me. They all seemed to be talking at the same time.

"You saved the game, Spin! You saved the game!" That was Chan, sounding nervous.

"Wall of Pain, Spin! Wall of PAIN!" That was Chris Fedorek.

"Don't worry, Spin, we'll still go for pizza. We'll *still...go...for...pizza.*" That was Frey, booming right next to my ear and squeezing my arm painfully hard.

Did I mention I was bleeding all over the ice? There is a ton of blood in a head, I discovered. You'd think it would deflate or something, but it didn't. The blood that didn't gush out onto the ice welled up in my mouth, leaving that awful, metallic blood taste.

A lot of the guys started to look sick and turned away. Mr. Bruseker power-skated over to me with an ice pack, spraying me with shaved ice as he came to a perfect power-skating stop. Mr. O'Donnell and Ms. Fong struggled onto the ice in their boots and covered me with coats until the ambulance came.

I lay there with my shaved head and my bloody broken nose and my bloody split lip and thought that I'd done a pretty good job of making sure I couldn't model with Chad and Clarissa the next day.

And I'd done it without even trying!

I started to laugh. Somehow, at that moment, it all seemed very, very funny. Hilarious, even. I laughed and shuddered and blew bloody nose bubbles.

"He's shaking! He's having a seizure or something," Danny blurted out.

Shay, who gets very faint at the sight of blood, I learned (interesting piece of information to store away), peered down at me. He looked horrified.

Then he leaned in closer and said, "What the...he's, he's LAUGHING!"

Shay's voice sounded really high and nervous and *amazed*.

He turned to the other guys and shrieked, "He's lying here with his face beat to a pulp, bleeding all over the place, and this *sick freak* is LAUGHING!"

CHAPTER TWENTY-FOUR

NOT EVEN LYING ABOUT BEING IN THE HOSPITAL

I've lied about being in the hospital so many times that it actually feels kind of familiar.

I lied about getting my appendix out. And my tonsils. And my wisdom teeth. And there was that unfortunate episode of the fake-infected ingrown toenail, but that was a mistake. That was before I became a semiprofessional liar. I kept forgetting which foot it was supposed to be and limping on the wrong side. I look back on that lie and just shake my head.

Stick to the basics, that's what I've learned. Anything out of the ordinary gets noticed. Too much detail is suspicious too.

Anyway, the hospital was pretty much like I'd imagined it. The beds with wheels, the smell of medicine, the doctors with white coats, the long, boring hallways painted in those hospital colors. Hospital blue-green. Hospital peachy-beige.

But being a patient wasn't at all what I'd imagined. I'd always thought it would be an exciting, dramatic adventure with doctors and nurses rushing around, praising you for your bravery, and friends and family offering you sympathy and candy. But it's actually more about needles, the smell of cleaner, boredom, lights on at night, bloody nose dressings and mushy food.

I will never eat applesauce again.

Oh, and the nurses weren't all in white. I thought that was some kind of a law or something. Turns out, they wear hoodies and uniforms in all sorts of colors and patterns. Who knew?

I was in a room with four beds. Slow week for sickness, I guess, because there was only one other kid and me. His name was Brandon, and he had just had an operation. He mostly slept and moaned. His mom and dad were really nice, cheerful people, so it couldn't have been anything serious.

Mom and Macy were both sitting beside my bed when I woke up. Macy looked terrible, huge and blotchy and red, with mascara and tears running down her cheeks. She had her hand over her mouth. Mom was very pale.

"Beauty Boy!" they both exclaimed with relief as my eyes fluttered open. I honestly think they expected me to be dead.

But hey, I promised you at the beginning of the book: nobody dies. It would really suck if I lied about that, wouldn't it? *And then, I died. From all the blood loss. The end.*

"Ssshhhh," I said, pointing over at the next bed. Poor old Brandon's going to be telling his family that he shared a room with "Beauty Boy" and his family will say "That's nice, honey" and then seriously worry about him and talk to the doctors about adjusting his medications. Mom stood up and pulled the big curtain around my bed, like that would keep Macy's booming voice in.

"Oh, look at your poor, beautiful face," Macy whispered hoarsely, starting to cry again. Macy's whisper was another person's shout.

I got Mom to find a mirror, and I looked at my face. I did look pretty rough. Actually, I looked like a dollar-store Halloween mask, like something that would scare small children. I had two black eyes. The rest of my face was one big blackish-bluish bruise, and there was a line of black stitches down my swollen upper lip. My nose was swollen to probably twice its normal size. My chin had a big red scrape. Oh, yeah, and I was bald.

"How do you feel?" Mom whispered. She looked very worried.

I tried to speak, but my voice was just a croak. Mom held out a glass of water with a straw in it. Drinking was quite a challenge, because I had to breathe through my mouth. I dribbled disgustingly.

"You had emergency surgery on your nose and some stitches on your lip, and you got a concussion," Mom explained as I snorted and tried to suck through the straw. She teared up. "Oh, BB, you're a mess!"

"I seem to have a slight scrape," I said. Well, actually, what I said was more like "Oy sheem doo hab a shlide shgrabe," but Mom and Macy understood. They burst out laughing.

It was a lame family joke. My dad, apparently, once came in from some yardwork with a huge cut all down his arm, only noticing it when Mom screamed that he was bleeding. "I seem to have a slight scrape," he said and went off to get fourteen stitches. Anyway, Macy stopped crying so loudly.

"This boy," she declared to the entire hospital, wiping her eyes on a grubby hankie, "this boy is such a brave guy! The bravest, most generous guy in the world!" Good old Macy. She's kind of clued out about a lot of things, but she's really not so bad.

"Thanks, Macy," I croaked. I was barely understandable, but I'll translate for you. "Sorry about the shoot."

Macy looked guilty and turned away.

"Luke," said Mom, "Macy's new client is going to cover that shoot for you. We're done with shoots. Everything's settled. No more modeling. Macy had no idea how you really felt, and neither did I. Tell Macy this is what you want, because she needs to hear it from you."

"Oh, yeah, it's what I want, Macy. Seriously," I said. Then I thought I'd better make this completely clear while I was a sad and beat-up kid in a hospital bed. "I never want to model again. Ever again. Ever."

Macy leaned over and grabbed me in a very painful hug. She's a strong lady, and did I mention I was bruised and had lost a *ton* of blood? I felt weak when she let me go, and I kind of slid, bonelessly, back onto the pillows.

"Oh, Beauty, we had such great times! So many! You've been such a STAR! Remember being King of the Toddlers? Or Santa's Cutest Elf?"

Does the humiliation never stop?

Yes, at three years old I was crowned King Toddler in the Eastview Mall fashion show. We still have the tiny cape and crown to prove it, if you can actually imagine I'd make something like that up. And, yes, little-known Christmas fact: I was also Santa's Cutest Elf when I was seven. Ho, ho, ho.

Macy sat down heavily on the side of the bed, jarring my bruised arm with the IV in it.

I winced, but she was busy reminiscing.

"Oh, so much to remember, Beauty!" she sighed, shaking her head, the tears welling up again.

I wasn't concentrating too well, because she'd made such a slant in the bed that I was struggling not to roll right into her.

"I guess I gotta say sorry, BB," she said, looking down at her huge hands, clasped in her lap. "I thought your getting all crabby lately was just...you know... teenage stuff. Attitude. Hormones! I thought you were just frustrated with all the piddly little shoots, waiting for me to get you that big campaign that you deserved."

My mom, who was standing by the window, said, "We should have figured out why you were so unhappy, Luke. I'm sorry too."

I'd have appreciated all of this much more if I hadn't been bumping and jolting to Macy's every move.

"But all good things come to an end, as they say, right?" said Macy. "You'll always be my little BB, and

I'll always be your auntie who loves you…" She kissed my bald head, got up and stumbled from the room.

"Ummm, what was all that about?" I asked.

"Macy's feeling bad," Mom explained, sitting down on the chair by the bed. "Models by Macy is really taking off. She's already got that new client. I think you know him. Cody something-or-other. Anyway, she's decided to move to Toronto. Where the action is, she tells me. But I think she feels like she's letting you down."

Letting me down? Letting me *down*? The relief was huge. I hoped Models By Macy would be a huge, huge success. I hoped Cody would do a movie and make himself and Macy a million bucks. I told Mom to tell Macy that I wished her all the best. And the funny thing was, I did! She worked hard. She had a big heart. So long as I wasn't involved, I *did* wish her the best.

"Mom…" I said, struggling to sit up. My head pounded alarmingly, so I inched back down onto the pillow. "Mom," I whispered, "what about us? What are we going to do without the modeling money?"

"We'll be fine," Mom said, smiling. She looked happy and relaxed. I was glad to see it. I mean, her only child had almost died from blood loss, but I was glad to see she wasn't dwelling on it.

"I've had quite a day. I went to Red Plush this morning—had my résumé with me and this little speech planned about my retail experience and my business-admin course. Red says, 'Hey, Spin's Mom, you ever seen *All About Eve*? Pull up a chair, sweetie.'"

I smiled (which was more of a drooling grimace). That was so Red.

"Anyway, we spent the whole morning together, talking, watching old movies…She's wonderful…So, you're looking at the new manager of Red Plush (and associated properties)!"

"What?!" I exclaimed, sitting up. A pulse of pain shuddered through my head. I sank back down onto the pillow.

"What?" I whispered.

"It's true. I'll be managing Red Plush and all those apartment buildings across the park! I've already given notice at the card store," she smiled. "Felt good."

Wow. A lot can happen when you're bleeding all over a hockey rink. This was almost too good to be true.

"And that's not all," she rushed on, clearly excited. "Since Red's son moved out of the basement suite in her house—you know, the big blue house next door to Red Plush, she offered it to us! She showed it to me and it's really cute. You'll love it. Small, but it's just a few blocks from school, the Freys live on that street, and there's that park where you and the Frey boys play hockey…"

I have never seen her so excited. I lay back and watched her and listened to her plan. It really hurt to smile (and there was the drooling problem), but it was hard not to. Macy in Toronto, managing Cody, Mom managing Red Plush, me managing my own life. How could everything work out so well so quickly?

I fell asleep with Mom sitting there holding my hand. She was smiling big enough for both of us.

* * *

My class made cards for me. Most of them were standard get-well-sooners. Frey and Chan did one together. It had a crude, Sharpied hockey stick and puck on the front, and inside they wrote, *The Rink Is Waiting*. They didn't even sign it, but I knew who sent it.

Mrs. Walker had included a card of her own. It was one of those big, fancy metallic cards that cost about six dollars, from the kind of store my Mom works at (*oops*, used to work at!).

It said:

Dear Luke,

I'm very, very sorry for the accident and for your injuries. I feel badly about it. I've had a long talk with your mother, and I know the truth about your absences, and I think I understand why you lied to me about them. I have, however, arranged some volunteer work for you to do for the children's hospital when you get back.

Your junior-high family hopes you get well soon!

Sincerely,

Principal Margaret Walker

PS. *I've signed up for skating lessons!*

I know, I know. You're thinking I got off pretty lightly, aren't you? Monster lying, and then only having to do a little volunteer work? You're right. I owe Mrs. Walker big-time. Even though she broke my nose and split my lip, and there was a TON of blood (did I mention that?), I still owe her.

Shay's "card" was just a folded piece of loose-leaf. Inside, all it said was *Get better you Sick Freak*. That made me laugh. Maybe it's actually hard to be Shay.

My heart started thumping when I got to Edie's card. It was beautiful. She'd drawn a very detailed castle with a dragon wound around the top turret, its tail fins looking like the castle flags. Inside, it was like you'd opened the castle doors, and there was a banner that said *Welcome to the Kingdom*, and a view out of the high castle windows to forests and the sea. That card was so typical of Edie; I didn't really understand it, and it probably didn't mean anything very special to her, but it made me feel happy.

Something fluttered out of the card when I opened it, and I picked it up off the bed. It was a photo. I remembered that Edie had been one of the photographers for the FUNdraiser. It was a picture of me, number 13, skating away from the camera, hunched over my stick, looking like an actual hockey player.

On the back of the picture, Edie had written: *Hey, lucky* 13, *bring your nose in soon so we can feel the bump.*

It was a terrific picture, the only picture ever taken of me that I actually like.

I lay there holding the picture, staring out at the snow that was falling outside the hospital in the real non-hospital world. My whole body ached, my nine very ugly stitches in my very ugly upper lip were throbbing, and I couldn't breathe through my very swollen nose.

It was a strange time to think that life was just about perfect.

Sick Freak: The Luke Spinelli Story.

CHAPTER TWENTY-FIVE

BECOMING NORMAL: THE SORT-OF END OF THE LUKE SPINELLI STORY

After a few weeks of looking like Frankenstein's monster, I'm almost back to normal. My hair's grown in a bit. My bruises went from hideous purply-black to ghoulish blue to sickly greenish-yellow and then faded away. I can actually feel my face again, so I no longer drool disgustingly out of the side of my mouth without noticing it. The stitches are out of my upper lip, leaving a surprisingly small but very cool hockey-player-like scar. And even though the doctors yanked my nose all over the place to fix it, it's still a bit crooked.

I started volunteering at the hospital two days after I got out. Typically, it did not go as I had imagined. My imagination is never, ever right.

I had imagined myself wheeling sick, grateful little kids into the playroom, reading them funny books or pushing the snack trolley full of sugary treats. Pathetic, hey? And I'm not even getting into how I'd imagined diagnosing mystery illnesses that had baffled the best medical minds, performing emergency surgery and evacuating an entire unit from a raging chemical fire. Nope, I'll just leave it there.

Anyway, reality time. Most of my first volunteer shift was spent getting the hospital people to understand that I was not actually a patient. My face still being alarmingly hideous, they had me in a wheelchair and on the way to the emergency department before I knew what was happening.

Eventually, I did do some volunteer work. My job was Playroom Freak, and I did it well. I scared off several little sick kids from the playroom where I was tidying up toys and had to explain my messed-up face to some of the braver ones who stayed.

"Hockey injury," I said very casually. You *know* I'll be bragging about that my whole life long.

Even though my days of modeling are over, it still comes back to haunt me occasionally. For example, we got a catalog in the mail yesterday. Remember that modeling shoot I did with Clarissa and a bunch of other kids where Clarissa was being a real jerk? It was a few chapters back?

Remember how we were all fake-pointing and fake-laughing like fools at the amazing, astonishing, droopy, deflated purple balloon? Everyone but Clarissa. She's fake-smiling right into the camera, in the classic center-of-attention, look-at-me Clarissa pose.

Turns out, we're actually pointing and grinning at a big yellow circle that says *Seniors Get 15% off on Tuesdays!*

Pretty glamorous life I used to lead, hey?

In other modeling news, I got an email from Cody Radwanski yesterday.

Have you heard? Cody is the new face of McTavish Soup. It's a huge campaign: the whole North American market. Cody's the McTavish Soup Kid. You've probably seen the commercials. It's all quiet. The camera pans in from outer space down to Cody's face. He's eating soup. He finishes slurping a noodle, opens his huge blue eyes really wide and whispers blissfully, "Oodles of noodles!" Like he *really means it* (which he probably does). And a voiceover says, "McTavish Soup. It really matters."

Watch for big things from Cody.

So here's his email. It's so Cody.

Hi, Lukester, please tell me you aren't mad at me? I mean, for Macy moving out to Toronto and everything. She says you aren't mad. I hope you aren't.

I can't believe you quit modeling! You were awesome! The best! Don't you miss it? We had such awesome times, you, me and Chad. Remember the skateboarding shoot? AWESOME! I'll never forget you, Lukester. You were always there for me. A Best Friend Forever.

Hey, have you seen the Oodles of Noodles commercials? Macy got me that audition. I love that soup. It really DOES have oodles of noodles!

Macy's got Chad as a client now too! His mom is fine with it. He still has great hair. He's trying to break into the music industry. He did a YouTube video of a song he wrote called "Click It!" It's awesome! The next Justin Bieber!

Macy says she's got some movie auditions lined up for me. I'm thinking of changing my last name to Rad. Just Cody Rad, without the wanski. Tell me what you think.

I have to go to a shoot now. It's a holiday one. I love holiday shoots! I think it's Easter. Hope I find lots of eggs!

Cody

Good old Cody Rad (wanski). It was great to hear from him.

Macy emails regularly. Even in print, she's pure Macy, only quieter. Here's her latest:

Hugs and kisses from TO, BB! Hey, I got a lead on a sporty shoot that you'd be perfect for (the rugged look is coming back in too), so if you're having second thoughts, let me know. Tell your mom I'm sending out a check for you guys. Oodles of moola from the McTavish Soup campaign! Buy yourself a good hockey helmet, skates, the works, you jock you.

Love, Auntie Macy

Mom and I moved out of the Dead End Street duplex. We boxed up all the pictures of me and put them in Red's basement storage. Red's house is awesome. We've got our own separate apartment downstairs, but sometimes we get together with Red for dinner or a movie. Humphrey the bulldog has sort of adopted me and comes and goes in our apartment like he owns the place. He even sometimes sleeps in my bed. I take him for a walk every day. I get *paid* to have fun with a dog. I'm saving up for a bike.

Almost every day after school, I play hockey with Frey and his brothers. Mom found us some second-hand benches and a storage bin for all the gear, so we're practically semiprofessional.

Shay doesn't bug me anymore. Why? Who knows. Did the on-ice accident convince him that I was too tough? Too weird? Too sick-freakish? I'll never know. All I know is that the next person he picks on is going to have a little help from me.

* * *

Well, hey, you know what? I think we're almost done here.

Thanks for sticking with me through the whole book, even when I've been annoying and whiny. You've been great. I promise you this: I'll read the story of your life when you get around to writing it. I'm sure you have one. Everybody's got a story.

I have to stop now. Pizza's here.

Maybe you haven't heard. In the new, improved real world of Luke Spinelli, Saturday nights are pizza nights. With real soda and everything.

Okay, get up. I think we have time for one last pose.

Grab a piece of pizza. Hold it about an inch from your mouth. Close your eyes, breathe and smile. Hold that pose. Now bite aaaaannnd chew.

Repeat, even if nobody's watching.

Especially if nobody's watching.

ACKNOWLEDGMENTS

Thanks to my editor, Sarah Harvey, who made me laugh while making the book better. Thanks also to all my family for their kindness while I wrote this book, and especially to Kate, for understanding how even small stories matter.

ALISON HUGHES has lived, worked and studied in Canada, England and Australia. She started writing when it became clear that it was much more fun and flexible than law and didn't require her to wear nylons. She lives in Edmonton with her husband and three children; her three dogs and two cats are her writers' group. She has never been a child model and is much more comfortable behind the camera in family pictures.